HOW TO BE TRUE

Daisy May Johnson

GODWINBOOKS

HENRY HOLT AND COMPANY
NEW YORK

Henry Holt and Company, *Publishers since 1866*
Henry Holt® is a registered trademark of
Macmillan Publishing Group, LLC
120 Broadway, New York, NY 10271 • mackids.com

Our books may be purchased in bulk for promotional, educational,
or business use. Please contact your local bookseller or the Macmillan
Corporate and Premium Sales Department at (800) 221-7945 ext. 5442
or by email at MacmillanSpecialMarkets@macmillan.com.

Library of Congress Control Number: 2022908056

First edition, 2022

Designed by Trisha Previte

Printed in the United States of America by Lakeside Book Company,
Harrisonburg, Virginia

ISBN 978-1-250-84045-5 (hardcover)

1 3 5 7 9 10 8 6 4 2

THIS IS A STORY ABOUT THREE THINGS

1. A painting. It is called *Les Roses Blanches*, which, in English, means "The White Roses," and it is a very precious thing indeed. All paintings are precious, of course, but this one is particularly so. It has survived love and loss and the sort of sadness that can rest so deep inside your heart that you do not even know it is there.

2. Footnotes. If you have read one of my books before, you will know that I am very fond of footnotes. I am quite a forgetful sort[1] and footnotes allow me to fill in the bits that I remember later on. Every time you see a small number next to a word like this,[2] that means that there is a footnote for you to look at. They are usually on the bottom of the page unless Good Sister Gwendolyn[3] has

---

1 I am also very easily distracted by second breakfasts, elevenses, afternoon tea, supper, and midnight feasts. In my defense, Good Sister Honey really is a remarkable caterer.

2 This is a footnote. It is the second footnote on this page so go back up and find the first and then things will all make sense. Or, alternatively, just read the paragraph above this one. You are in charge!

3 You might be wondering who and indeed what a Good Sister is. They are nuns and they are rather fabulous. I should know, for I am also a nun. My name is Good Sister June, I am the headmistress of a very remarkable school, and I am very fond of a Victoria sponge. And that, my friends, is the sort of secret that a footnote is perfect for.

gotten a little overexcited when she's printed this out and then who knows where they're going to happen.

3. A very small and very revolutionary plant shop on the Rue de la Vérité, a street that is full of buns and pastries and rebellion and is located right in the heart of Paris.

A GIRL NAMED MARIANNE

When she was fourteen years old, Marianne Montfort had been sent out to find a job. She was not particularly happy about this, but she had not been happy about anything since her family had moved to France and left the country of her birth far behind. It was the sort of sadness that had begun to rule her every waking moment. She would find it talking to her as she laid the table for lunch, or whispering in her ear as she tried to make friends at school: *You do not belong here; this is not your home.*

Her parents knew about this sadness, for they had their own. Her father had started a new life teaching at a university in Paris and felt that somebody would tell him that they had made a mistake with every lecture he took or student he spoke to, and her mother had found a job in a local shop and bit her tongue when somebody pretended that they did not understand her accent or what she was saying to them. It was only the knowledge that their family was safe and together that kept their sadness and worries at bay.

Marianne's sadness, however, lingered. Her parents watched it wrap around her and slowly pull their daughter away from

1

the world. She began to stay inside the house and home from school, and every day saw her grow quieter and paler and stiller. And so they came to a decision: Marianne must be sent out to find a job that would distract her from her sadness and pull her back into the world.

And that was the day that she found a very small and very revolutionary plant shop on the Rue de la Vérité.[4]

A SMALL AND REVOLUTIONARY PLANT SHOP

The owner of the plant shop was called Madame Clement. She was a tall and big woman, full of power and strength and heart, and over the years they spent together she taught Marianne everything she knew about plants. She taught her how to bring a snowy orchid back to life with nothing but words, how to make the slate rose bloom for weeks on end, and how to make the iron lilies in their shop grow taller than anywhere else in the city. She taught her what chemists grow in their gardens,[5] what you call a nervous tree,[6] and why herbs are the most supportive plants of all.[7] And in between all of that, she taught Marianne how she could help make a better world.

"It's not that you have to make all of it better," said Madame Clement, as she nibbled on the end of a *pain au chocolat*.[8] "But you should try to make your little bit of it better. If everyone

....

5 Chemist trees.
6 A sweaty palm.
7 Because they are full of encourage-mint.
8 This is a type of pastry full of chocolate, and the fact that Madame Clement liked to eat them for her breakfast should tell you how good of an egg she really was.

does that for their little bits of the world, then just imagine what happens when all those little bits come together."

And so, as soon as they opened the shop, Madame Clement sent Marianne out to deliver flowers and plants to all of the other shop and restaurant owners on the Rue de la Vérité. The Italian brasserie run by old Signore Alberici[9] received a pot of silver thyme to flavor his meals while the young new owner of the chocolate shop, Madame Laurentis, received a bunch of roses as brightly colored as her hair. A random passerby on their way to work was given a plant to take into their office while the street cleaners received daffodils that were still wet with dew. There were some days that Marianne thought they might run out of things to sell because they'd given so much of it away, but the shelves of the shop never looked empty.

On the days that it rained or snowed, Marianne stayed inside the shop. In a way, she liked those days best, for she could learn directly from Madame Clement herself. She learned how Madame Clement gave shelter to students with nowhere else to go; how she pressed food into the arms of the homeless and helpless from the windows at the back of the shop; and watched as she helped the local school children plan their protest against the horrors of their new school menu.[10] Marianne helped Madame Clement clean out the cellar of the shop so that the single mothers could meet and let their children play in safety together; she watched as Madame Clement let

9   There was a rumor that he was about to retire and sell up to a nice young couple from Germany. As you will see shortly, he does and they are very nice indeed.

10   There was far too much kale, and nobody liked that.

the activists plan their revolutions in there in the evenings and allowed the street artists to store their kits inside the shop when it rained.

Every single second that Marianne spent with Madame Clement felt like a gift.

THE GREATEST OF ALL GIFTS

Madame Clement left the shop to Marianne in her will.

MARIANNE MONTFORT AND JEAN-CLAUDE BERGER

Marianne loved that shop so much that, on the day her parents told her they were moving to a new country and starting a new life all over again, she decided to stay in Paris. She had spent her life looking for somewhere she belonged, and the plant shop, with its windows full of sunlight and shelves full of green, had become precisely that. She packed it full of unusual and odd plants, the sorts of things that you could see nowhere else in Paris but there. She planted an Egyptian walking onion outside the front door and whenever it was picked, the scent of onions would roll down the Rue de la Vérité, whilst inside, ghost orchids and bat lilies and hundreds of other plants packed every inch of free space. In the middle of it sat Marianne like a queen, and she carried out Madame Clement's wishes for liberty and equality with all her heart. She let the feminist students meet for free in the room above the shop to plan their next adventures; helped the homeless find somewhere warm and safe for the night in the cellar below; and handed out biscuits to those who were lonely and asked them to stay and talk to her for a while.

On the rare occasions that Marianne's sadness tried to be

a part of this brave new world of hers, the light streaming in through the windows or the bright, fierce color of the bougainvillea made it fade away into nothing.

And then, one day, her sadness stopped coming entirely.

THE DAY THE SADNESS STOPPED

Jean-Claude Berger did not arrive at the plant shop on purpose.

He had turned left down a street that he had thought looked familiar before realizing that it was not, and only stubbornness and the sight of his family's château, perched high on the hill in the distance like some tempting fruit from a tree, kept him going. But the streets of Paris were against him, and they kept twisting away from the château and taking him somewhere else. A brasserie spilling out onto the pavement; three old men playing belote with each other outside their homes; a row of bicycles locked to each other; and then the Seine, the river itself, glinting in the bright sunlight. A perfect city to be lost in, at a perfect time.

In many ways, Jean-Claude was content with being lost, for he knew that it was only through being lost that you can find yourself. He had spent many years at a dark and gray school in England, where the boys were very good at being lonely and not very good at making friends with each other. He had been sent there by his grandmother following the death of his parents. Odette Berger[11] had not known what else to do with the small

----

11 Remember this name. She is Very Important.

9

and bright-eyed child who had been presented to her, and so she had sent him away in the hope that others might know better. But the school was strange and sad and cold, and all too fond of serving the children kale.[12]

Jean-Claude had not enjoyed it one bit. He had kept himself happy and sane by fighting back against the authorities wherever he could. He protested everything from the presence of broccoli soup on the menu through to the mandatory cold showers after PE. The staff had responded to his rebellions in the only ways they knew how: lines, detentions, sending him to bed without supper, and, after Jean-Claude had climbed onto the roof and unfurled a banner that said THIS SCHOOL IS NOT NICE on Visitors' Day, expelling him.

And expulsion was the best thing that could have happened to Jean-Claude, for it set him free.

---

12 And if this does not give you an idea of how horrible it was, then nothing will.

THE FREEDOM OF
JEAN-CLAUDE BERGER

When the school telephoned her, Odette sent Jean-Claude the money to return home. He refused it, for a part of him wanted to discover the world upon his own terms and without the help of his privileged family behind him. He went to London and found a job and then a room, paying with the last handful of money he had to his name, and it was there that he learned about a world that he didn't even know existed. He went to meetings and lectures held by people who were making a difference in the world, and realized that he wanted to do the same. He wanted to use his money to help people. He wanted to make a difference with it.

And so, at last, he began to make his long and slow way back to Paris to do precisely that.

When he found himself lost on the Rue de la Vérité, he did not realize that his future wife was there to greet him. Of course, Marianne did not know this either. All that she knew was that a young man had stopped to study the window of the plant shop where a row of quite delightful tiny plants and equally delightful feminist slogans[13] jostled for attention.

After a while, he nodded to himself as if satisfied, and came into the shop.

---

13 "Plants, Not Patriarchy" and "Bloom for Yourself and Not for Others" and "Make Compost, Not War."

PICKING THE RIGHT POTTED PLANT

"I wish to purchase a present for my grandmother," said the man with bright blue eyes to Marianne. "I've been away from home but now I'm back. Your display caught my eye and I thought that a plant might be a good idea. I don't know what to pick. She's kind of difficult to buy for. There's only the two of us, and I've been gone for a while and . . . you don't need to know all of that. Do you have any suggestions?"

Marianne nodded. The giving of plants was a slow and quiet thing, one that took time and thought, and so she played for both by asking him about the weather. And then his journey. And why he'd been away. They were small and vague questions to ask and she was not bothered by them nor the answers he gave. What mattered was the way he gave them, and the way he looked as he did so.

When he finished speaking, Marianne picked out two plants and put them on the counter between them. One of them was perfect and one of them was not. The perfect one was called Heloise and had been grown from a cutting from one of Madame Clement's most beloved and elderly specimens. Marianne had not thought that Heloise would survive, for she had turned brown and then yellow and after all of that, her leaves had begun to curl up at the ends. She had moved her around the shop from sunlight to shade, trying to find the best place for her and failing miserably. It was only when Marianne had placed her on a shelf with a direct and uninterrupted view of the world outside that Heloise had been happy. She was a plant who needed adventure and this man, Marianne knew, would give her that.

"One of these," she said. "Either one will be fine."

He picked the right one.

Of course he did.

THE HEART OF THE MATTER

Their daughter was born nine short months later. Her fists were balled tight as she came into the world and her eyes were bright with fire and life.

She was a baby born to change the world, and they named her Edmée Agathe Aurore Berger.

Or Edie, for short.

A REVOLUTIONARY CHILDHOOD

Edie Berger learned what a protest was before she could talk. She went to one when she was just three days old, a tiny ball of noise and fire, wrapped in the arms of her mother and surrounded by thousands of other voices. Many other babies might have found the experience upsetting, but Edie found it exciting. It was like growing up in the middle of a whirlwind and knowing that she was in control of it all. She learned how to read people and understand everything that they didn't know they were sharing. By the time she was four, Edie could spot the signs of danger in a crowd of people,[14] and how to get out of trouble before trouble even realized she was in it. By the time she was five, she could navigate her way around the city with her eyes (metaphorically) closed. She knew all of the bakers and the patisseries and which of them was the best at

....

14 "What you have to understand is that there's a moment where people stop thinking about what they *should* be thinking about, and start thinking about something else entirely. And the problem comes when they start thinking about the *wrong* thing." And because this is possibly the clearest thing I have ever heard Edie say, I have included it here in its entirety.

making bread and who could put together the most beautiful macarons.

Sometimes people who did not know Edie would grow concerned about her well-being. A small girl purposefully walking down the street by herself, with hair the size of a wild storm cloud, would always attract attention. But whenever these people walked toward her, the shopkeepers and locals would intervene and tell them that it was all right. Everybody knew Marianne and Jean-Claude, and everybody knew their daughter. Edie was safer there than anywhere else in the world. Madame Laurentis would give her a handmade chocolate as Edie wandered past her small and perfectly formed sweetshop, and a history book for Jean-Claude to read. Frau and Herr Bettelstein, freshly arrived from Germany and running the brasserie of their dreams,[15] pushed fresh *apfelstrudel*[16] into Edie's hands and an order for roses from Marianne. And on the days when everybody was too busy in their shops and restaurants, old Monsieur Abadie would fold his paper and rise from the bench[17] at the end of the Rue de la Vérité and escort Edie back home to the plant shop.

----

15 Signore Alberici had, at last, retired and sold his brasserie. He had gone off in a camper van to tour the world, selling pizzas at the roadside to fund his travels. If you ever are lucky enough to come across him, I particularly recommend his spinach and ricotta pizza.

16 A particularly delicious pastry involving apples, sugar, and lots of love. Good *apfelstrudel* comes from the heart, and the one that the Bettelsteins made was one of the best in the entire world.

17 The bench was dedicated to Lizette, which was a name that meant nothing to the neighborhood, but I shall tell you: It was the first name of Madame Clement. Lizette Clement had been somebody whom Monsieur Abadie

Although they all had rooms at the family château way up on the hill, Edie and her parents tended to sleep in the basement of the plant shop, the three of them wrapped up in rugs and cushions and caring for nothing other than being together. Each night, Jean-Claude would tell his small daughter bedtime stories of the brave and remarkable women in France. He spoke of people like Joan of Arc, and of George Sand and Louise Michel, and even though Edie did not quite understand everything that he said, she knew that the stories made her heart sing.

"But that's what they *should* do," Jean-Claude said when Edie told him this. He gave her a little squeeze of pride. "Stories don't just stay inside a book. You carry everything you've read inside of you, and when you need them, it's the memory of those stories that will help you figure out what to do with your life."

And when he said that, Edie realized that she was going to change the world.

"I'm going to change the world," said Edie.

"Quite right, too," said Jean-Claude. "I'd expect nothing less."

....

had loved very much, and she had loved him back. He had paid for the dedication himself and had it put on the bench one night when nobody was around. And every morning when he sat there with his newspaper, he thought of the girl he had loved and his heart became full with a fresh-found joy because of it.

LIKE OIL AND WATER

Throughout all of this, Edie's great-grandmother[18] was kept at a distance. It was not that Edie did not want Odette to be in her life, or that Jean-Claude did not want Odette to be in his, but it was more the fact that none of them quite knew how to do it. They tried, of course, in that rather complicated and not-very-useful way that adults tend to do such things. Jean-Claude would help Odette by picking up her shopping and Odette would say thank you by inviting him, Marianne, and Edie every weekend for lunch. And even though they always went, none of them enjoyed it.

"It is necessary," said Marianne when Edie told her how she felt. "I know it's awful, but you have to get to know her. Odette is the only family that you have in this country other than us. My parents are halfway around the world. You need to know

18 Technically Odette is Edie's great-grandmother, but as Jean-Claude's parents were not alive, they had always called each other grandmother and granddaughter. Admittedly they had also called each other a lot of other names, but because some of them were less than polite, I shall not repeat them here however much Edie might want me to. (Yes, she is standing right behind me as I write. Yes, she *should* be going to her lessons instead.)

who will look after you here, in case something ever happened to us. Do you know what I mean by that?"

"I do understand your point, but also I do not want to," said Edie with great honesty.

"That's good enough for me," said Marianne. "Come and help me deadhead the daffodils."[19]

And so that was the end of it: Odette was in Edie's life, and Edie would be in hers, even though neither of them liked it one bit. Odette did not like the way her granddaughter walked, or the way she talked. She insisted on calling her Edmée, which was as foreign to Edie as flying; she did not like the way Edie sat,[20] or the stories that she read, and she definitely did not like the fact that Edie was going to follow her parents into activism when she grew up.

"Activism isn't a career," Odette said when she learned this.

"Neither is being horrible," said Edie, when she heard this.

"Would you like some more peas?" said Jean-Claude, when he deliberately ignored all of this.

Edie did not like the way her grandmother kept rooms in the château locked from anybody but her. She did not like the way that Odette spoke about the priceless paintings in her collection but refused to show them to anybody. Art was not for hiding in Edie's world. It was for propping up on the walls of the plant shop and letting the young babies who could barely hold a pen draw on it. It was for helping people see the possibilities

....

19 This sounds very dramatic but it is just pulling the dead bits off the plant and leaving the live bits on.

20 Odette was fond of people who sat quietly in the corner and didn't get into any trouble whatsoever. It will shock you to discover that Edie was not—and never would be—one of these people.

of the world that they lived in. Nobody could see the possibilities of Odette's art collection. She had let one writer in to view it and make a book about it, but that had been years ago. Anytime Edie even as much as looked at the room, Odette clicked the lock shut and placed the key in her pocket.

On one particularly frustrating day, Edie had asked her father about it. "Have you ever been in that room?" She had watched Odette go carefully into the room and close the door behind her. When Edie had tried to open it, the door had been locked.

"Yes," said Jean-Claude. "A long time ago. Does it really matter, though? Everyone must have secrets, and that room clearly holds hers."

"But I want to know what's in it," said Edie. "And even though you are quite reasonable and calm-sounding right now, I think you want to know as well."

Jean-Claude shrugged. "I did," he said. "But now I want to know so much more than that. The world is an expanse. It waits for us all. 'Awake, arise or be for ever fall'n.'"[21]

It was the sort of reply that didn't make sense. It was also the sort of reply that bordered on being slightly irritating. And his daughter was not the sort of person to let that go without comment. "That doesn't make sense," said Edie. "Also, it borders on being slightly irritating."

"It will make sense," said Jean-Claude.

And on one too-soon day, it did.

....

21 This is a quote from a very long and occasionally very brilliant poem called *Paradise Lost*. It is quite complicated to read, however, so I recommend waiting a few years and then making sure that you've got a custard cream on hand.

LIKE LEAVING HALF YOUR HEART BEHIND

"I'm sorry," said Marianne. "Things are . . . complicated."

"You should be sorry. You're leaving me behind," said Edie. She glared fiercely at her parents. "You are going abroad and leaving me behind, and what is worse, you are leaving me with *her*. That does not feel complicated at all." A part of her felt like crying, but another, much more interesting part felt like throwing a lot of things onto the ground and jumping upon them. She was only stopped from doing this when her father raised his eyebrows at her. She could tell that he didn't understand her reaction. Sometimes her parents could understand the feelings of everybody but her. It was one of the problems of having parents who were so good at what they did.[22]

"Tell me what you're thinking," said Jean-Claude, who was

....

22 If this sentence does not convince you of Edie's raw and wonderful and unrelenting love for her parents, then I do not know what does. As she told me once, they were idiots but they were *her* idiots, and that was what mattered more than anything else on the earth. (And then, because she had been far too sincere for too long, she threw a stink bomb at a passing first-year before climbing out of the nearest window.)

also very good at realizing that Edie wanted to say something and didn't know where to begin.

"I am thinking that sometimes I wish you were not so good at what you do," said Edie.

"We are only good because we have the money and the time and the resources to *be* good at what we do. I spent years hating everything that my family had until I realized what good we could do with it. We can use all of those resources and the time and the money to make the world a better place.

"There are people who need somebody to help them, and we can do that. Not many people have that chance, but we do. We can support the people who need help and give them anything they need. We can be there for them when nobody else is. We can help to fight the battles that they need to fight.

"But your mother is right. All of this comes at a price. We are going to be visiting places all around the world, and not all of them will be safe . . ."

"I can look after myself," said Edie, interrupting.

"I know,"[23] said Marianne, "but we're going to be working with activist organizations all around the world. Armies, too. Some of the things we do may be dangerous. They will not be safe. And we won't be able to do any of that if we're worrying about you. Odette will look after you. She is your family."

It is in such moments that the world can be torn apart, and so it was with Edie.

And even though she did not quite believe it was true or that

....

23 There were many doubtful things inside Marianne's mind, but the one thing she did not doubt was the remarkable strength of her daughter.

it would all happen (for her parents were particularly talented at planning schemes that did not always work out) it was only a week later that she found herself standing on the front doorstep of the château.

Saying goodbye.

HOW TO SAY THE IMPOSSIBLE

Marianne bent down and wrapped her arms around her daughter and squeezed her very tight. "Remember this," she said, with her face buried in Edie's hair. "Remember the way that this feels, that it is *me*; remember that, even if you forget all else." And after a long while, when neither of them spoke or even remembered what words were, Marianne stood up and walked toward the waiting taxi. She did not look back. I do not think that she could, not with half her heart left behind her.

Jean-Claude touched his daughter's face with his hand and looked deep into her eyes. "You must represent everything about us while we are gone," he said. "You must be true to yourself and to us. It might seem like forever but I promise it isn't. Time is just a blink of an eye. The hours will pass. The weeks will fly by. And as soon as we can, we will come home and be together again."

It was then that it all became real.

Too, too real.

"Let me come," Edie said in a voice that nobody heard, not even herself. She said it again as Odette and Jean-Claude embraced and said farewell,[24] and she said it again as Jean-Claude got into the taxi. She said it again as the engine started up and then she found herself repeating it constantly, softly, painfully, all the way until the taxi had driven down the hill and out of view.

And then she did not say anything else, for there was nothing left to say.

---

24 Sometimes adults do tend to do what they think they must do, rather than what their heart tells them. This moment between Jean-Claude and Odette was precisely that. And the fact that they did not tell each other the truth about how they were feeling is perhaps the saddest moment in this entire book.

THE NEW WORLD OF EDIE BERGER

And so, a new life began for Edie even though she was neither ready nor willing nor able to receive it.

The plant shop was given over to the care of Isabelle Tremont, a friend of Marianne's, and Edie was given a bedroom on the top floor of the château. It was surrounded by empty and abandoned rooms; some of them full of furniture that had been forgotten for many years, and others packed full of nothing more than long and lace-like cobwebs. It was a space that was perfect for adventure, but Edie could not see it then. She was far too busy nursing her broken heart and trying to ignore the fact that every day she spent without her parents made it break a little bit more.

It did not help that life with her grandmother was complicated at best. Odette was an early riser, fond of being awake for hours before the sunlight, and there were some days when Edie did not even see her. She would climb down the long and lonely stairs and be given her breakfast in the dining room, and she would spend hours wandering around the house until somebody remembered her lunch and then somebody else remembered her dinner. And throughout all of that, Odette wouldn't be anywhere to be seen.

Edie knew where she was, of course. Everybody did. Odette would go to the safety and silence of her art collection, and each time she did, the door was firmly locked behind her. She would spend hours there by herself with the paintings and sculptures and when Edie tried to ask her about it, Odette would close up and change the subject. She would say "Have you done your homework?" on a Saturday, or "Have you had your supper?" when it was only just eleven in the morning and so, eventually, Edie stopped asking and began to sneak out of the house instead.

The first time that she did it, Edie did not quite know what to do with herself. The city was so indelibly marked with the memories of her parents that a part of her did not want to go into it, and yet another, greater part made her start to walk in the direction of the Rue de la Vérité.

Madame Laurentis was the first to greet Edie. She raced out of her shop and gave her a heartfelt hug and a box of chocolates. "Keep them to yourself," she advised. "I will send chocolates up to the château for your grandmother, but these are all for you. Sometimes we should treat ourselves first, and you, my dear child, look as if you need a treat more than most." She was not wrong. All of the other shop owners saw the changes in Edie and reacted the only way that they knew how. Frau and Herr Bettelstein gave her some freshly baked rye bread sprinkled with caraway seeds on top. "It is my favorite," said Frau Bettelstein, smiling conspiratorially at Edie. "Everything is better when you have fresh bread, I think." Monsieur Abadie even escorted Edie back to the gate of the château and pressed a slab of toffee into her hand. "As I am an adult, I must tell you not to eat this before your meals," he said quietly. "But I would not listen to me. I have known a lot of stupid adults and only a handful of stupid children. You, my child, are not one of them."

And between them, Madame Laurentis and the Bettelsteins and Monsieur Abadie managed to keep Edie going. They handed food out to her every time they saw her,[25] and pretended to not notice when she had a tiny cry in the back of their shops or wiped her eyes in the windows of the brasserie. They were good people and they were enough to make Edie's long and lonely nights in the château feel bearable.

But nothing good lasts forever, and the Rue de la Vérité began to change. Monsieur Abadie went into hospital for his long-awaited operation, and his bench turned cold and empty without him. The brasserie grew busier and busier, and all that Herr and Frau Bettelstein could do was smile at Edie as they rushed past her. The chocolate shop suddenly became famous thanks to the review of a local writer, and so customers began to queue out of the doorway, each and every day, and all Madame Laurentis could do was wave at Edie as she walked past the shop's window.

And as the sadness began to build inside her heart once more, Edie decided to deal with things in the only way she knew how.

....

25 I feel like I must emphasize here that Odette was not starving Edie. Far from it. Edie had three very good meals a day and all the in-between meals that she liked. In a way, the food that she was given on the Rue de la Vérité was not really food at all. It was a way for people to tell her that they loved her and cared for her, and I think there is nothing more beautiful than that.

THE COPING MECHANISMS OF
EDIE BERGER

- Accidentally-on-purpose rappelling down the side of the Eiffel Tower. *Technically* Edie could have waited for the lifts to be fixed and stayed with her class on the viewing platform, but *technically* has never been a strength of hers.
- Accidentally-on-purpose sneaking her own paintings into the Louvre, a very prestigious and rather wonderful museum that was not quite ready for a lot of pictures all about macarons. *Technically* you and I might think of this as just a lot of circles but Edie has asked me to tell you that they were, in fact, exact replicas of the macarons in the Ladurée shop on the Champs-Élysées and you must visit there the next time you are in Paris or else she won't talk to you anymore.
- Accidentally-on-purpose taking her friends to London for a day trip when they *technically* should have been playing on the school playground rather than making their way to Buckingham Palace. Edie has asked me to point out that *technically* she did invite the staff to come with them and it isn't her fault that they weren't listening.[26]

....

26 An elementary error. One should always listen to small girls. It tends to save time.

THE FINAL STRAW

All of this did not improve things between Edie and Odette. I am not sure that it would have improved relationships for anybody, much less two people who were not quite sure what to do with each other in the first place. Odette experimented with grounding Edie, and with taking things away from her, and restricting her access to macarons, but nothing worked. At least, it didn't work for long. Edie simply coped with the punishment before continuing to live her life in precisely the manner she wanted. She would climb out of the windows if Odette locked the door, and when Odette locked the windows, Edie unlocked them again in a heartbeat.

The final straw came on a cold and wet autumn afternoon.[27] Odette had gone to her paintings, as she often did in times of trouble and stress, and Edie had been wandering around the top floor of the château, trying to figure out what to do with herself. This was a particularly challenging thing for anybody

....

27 I have come to realize that many things in books happen when the weather is Doing Something Exciting. For example, it is either a perfect winter's day and a fresh snowfall, or a perfectly bright summer afternoon, and I do not think this is very accurate. Most of the very interesting things in the world happen when it is at its dullest.

to do, let alone a particularly brilliant nine-year-old girl. It was too wet for her to go out and do things in the city. Even the most ambitious tourist had long since given up and the streets were gray and empty. The Rue de la Vérité was deserted and all the shops had closed hours ago. For all intents and purposes, Edie was stuck inside the house.

She went to the top floor of the south wing and then pushed open a window to get out onto the roof. Her feet skidded slightly as she got out there, but that didn't concern her. The secret was to not think about falling, and then one didn't. It was one of the first things Jean-Claude had taught her, as the two of them chased each other across the rooftop and left Marianne to talk to Odette.

"If you think of the worst thing to happen, then it most likely will," Jean-Claude had said, balancing very neatly on the top of a gargoyle, just as he had done when he had been a child at the château. "What you should do is think about the solution instead. For example, your dear mama could bring us home a coconut sponge[28] from the shop but instead I talk about the wonders of a meringue, and *voilà*. She brings us meringues, and coconut does not darken our door."

It was an impeccable argument, and one that Edie held to her heart every time she climbed out onto the roof. She took a moment to remember the soft and gentle smile of her father, before she walked out onto the tiles. She kept her feet balanced

---

28 I am sorry but coconut is the worst of all of the cakes, and I will not have any disagreements over this. Coconut-flavored anything is worse than raisins and kale and unexpected jam in chocolate cake altogether.

on either side of the roof, just where it came to a fine and sharp point, and headed all the way over to another window in the east wing. It was a favorite route of hers, for it allowed her to see all round the château and down into Paris itself. Sometimes she would come out on an evening when the moon was full and watch the lights of Paris glowing in the distance.

And even though it was raining and the roof was cold and tight with rain on this day in particular, it did not stop her from unlocking the window and carefully easing it open.

What did stop her, however, was the man who was breaking into her château.

THE MAN WHO SHOULDN'T HAVE BEEN THERE

It did not take Edie very long to get down from the roof. She slid down three drainpipes, hopped over a broken piece of gutter, and apologized to some birds as she skidded past their nest before finally swinging into her still-open bedroom window. Once there, she raced out into the corridor and toward the stairs; and then, several banister slides (and one slightly complicated bend where the stairs doubled back on themselves) later, she was down on the ground floor and heading straight for the painting room.

There was nowhere else in the château that the thief might go. Edie herself had spent weeks crafting a key to let herself in, determinedly filing down the edges and making it follow the pattern of the key that Odette carried around her neck. She was there every time her grand-mère opened the door and wore an expression of supreme innocence as she memorized the shape and look of the key, before she headed off back to her room to work furtively on a copy.

She pulled the key out of her pocket and studied the door thoughtfully. It was not how she had intended to test it, but it couldn't wait. She put the key into the lock and held her breath as she turned it gently to the side. There was a brief and awful moment when it felt like it might stick but then, smooth as butter, the lock gave and the door opened.

And she stopped, for she could not believe what she was seeing.

Every inch of the room was full of paintings. Pictures were packed together on the walls, and statues and sculptures crowded every corner. There was a small space in the middle for a sofa and an armchair, both of them looking at the same point in the wall, but that was it. It made Edie a little claustrophobic; there was so much *stuff* packed into this tiny, tiny room, and all of it had a gleam that told her it had cost a fortune.

Suddenly she felt cold air touch her skin.

One of the windows on the other side of the room fell forward onto the carpet.

And the man began to climb inside the house.

A LITTLE BIT OF DETAIL

The man's real name is Raphael, but you shall not know him as that for quite some time. He is small and slender and bendy, because he is a thief and sometimes thieves need to get into complicated places. He would not recommend being a thief because it is quite stressful and sometimes the jobs take a lot longer than you expect them to and sometimes cauliflowers get involved—

Wait. I shall tell you about those things in a while.

Especially the cauliflowers.

What I shall tell you about now is that Raphael is very fond of sausage sandwiches with a vast amount of ketchup on them, ice creams with two chocolate flakes in them, and making little patterns with the anchovies on his pizza. Many of these activities take place behind closed doors because, in public, he makes a great effort to be very boring. He wears the sort of clothes that you see on a thousand other men of his age, and nothing is too bright or too eye-catching. His brown hair is always cut very close to his head and when he needed glasses, he decided to get contact lenses instead so that people would not be able to tell the police about them.

Essentially, he looks about as interesting as a dry rice cake with kale on top and that, my friends, is not very interesting whatsoever.

Also, he is not great at thinking under pressure.

HOW TO STOP A THIEF

"Hello," said Edie.

"Hello," said the man, unable to stop himself.

"What are you doing here?"

"Cleaning," he said. "I'm the cleaner."

"The cleaner's name is Victoire, and you aren't her."

"I'm her replacement."

"What's your name?"

"Victor," he said.

Edie gave him a little *Was That Really the Best You Could Come Up With?* look. "Do you always clean houses by climbing in through the windows, Victor?"

"No," said Victor.[29]

"Aha," said Edie with some satisfaction. "Then you are a burglar."

"Yes," said Victor. "A little bit. Sorry."

"But what if I don't want you to burgle us?" said Edie. "Burgling is taking things from other people without asking, and

....

29 His name is Raphael in real life, as you know, but I shall call him Victor here because that is what Edie knew him as. Then.

you shouldn't do that. Even if they *are* quite old and very annoying."

"Oh," said Victor.

"Also," said Edie, "I have phoned the police."

"Oh," Victor said in a very different tone of voice. "In that case, then, I might have to not clean today." He took a step back and looked toward the window.[30] "In fact, I think I definitely won't be able to. Something has come up."

"That is fine," said Edie. She heard a soft little creak on the stairs behind her and realized that she was about to be joined by somebody else. It was somebody who sounded very much like Odette. Victoire made a sort of more purposeful, clunking sound because she usually had a vacuum in her hands, whilst all of the other staff were far away in the château kitchens and preparing dinner. "Victor—if you wait just a moment, I will introduce you to my grand-mère. I think she is coming to join us. She is very old but—"

Alas, we shall never know how Edie was going to finish that sentence, for the moment that Odette had entered the room, Victor had climbed out of the window and disappeared across the lawn. "That is disappointing," said Edie, watching him go. "But I think that it is all handled now. Nothing to worry yourself about, Grand-Mère, nothing at all! It is over."

But the look on Odette's face said something quite different.

It wasn't over.

Not at all.

....

30 To be precise, he looked at where the window had once been.

WHAT ODETTE SAID

"This is the last straw, Edmée.

"You're going away to school."

THE BEGINNING OF THE REST OF YOUR LIFE

And so Edmée Agathe Aurore Berger was sent away to school in the hope that she would, at last, become the prim and proper young lady that her grandmother longed for her to be.

The school that Odette chose really did look like it might be able to do this sort of thing.

It was called the School of the Good Sisters, and it was a boarding school that was run by nuns and located far away from any major transport hubs and sources of potential mayhem for her small granddaughter to exploit. The pictures of the school itself looked particularly promising. A thick layer of ivy blanketed the front wall of the school, while a tall iron railing wrapped around it like a too-tight shoelace, and the front door looked like something that a horror film would reject for being too scary. The roofs were flat, but broken up every now and then by tall and angular towers which can look more than a little bit like shadowy fingers reaching up into the sky.

Appearances, however, can be deceptive, and even though a substantial part of the building does not quite work as it should, and the leaks in the fifth-form science room have been there so long that they have come to support a specialist habitat of small and quite delightful orchids, and the doors into the kitchens do not technically lock as they should, the School of the Good Sisters is the best place in the world.

A WET AND RAINY WELCOME

Of course, Edie did not think this when she arrived at the school. The weather was cold and wet, and there was a slightly damp feeling in her shoes where the rain had gotten through. She had been put on the train in Paris by Odette and I think, if you asked Edie to tell you any part of that journey after that point, she would tell you that she does not remember.

But I think she does.

Sometimes we are able to make ourselves not remember the things that hurt the most. And that journey hurt. It was dark, and when she got to the station she was greeted by a woman who looked a little bit like a penguin.

The woman who looked a little bit like a penguin was Good Sister June,[31] and she was the headmistress of the School of the Good Sisters. She had been led to expect something different from the small and rather sad French girl that she found at the station, and so her first words were not what she had intended them to be. "Are you Edmée Berger? Are you really?"

....

[31] And just in case you've forgotten: Good Sister June is me. Don't tell anybody else.

45

She corrected herself almost immediately and said, "I mean, I'm your headmistress, and I know you *are* Edmée, but I'm just—I thought you might have somebody with you. It's not often I pick up the first-years by themselves."

"My grandmother stayed in Paris," said Edie.

Good Sister June raised her eyebrows. "Did you travel all the way here by yourself?"

"I do a lot of things by myself," Edie said after a long pause. She said it in English as well, even though it sounded ridiculously strange. None of the words felt right upon her tongue. "And my name's *Edie*. Not Edmée. I don't want to be called that anymore."

"Once upon a time I wanted to be called Victoria," said Good Sister June. "Not because I like the queen, but rather because I am enormously fond of the cake. Do you have a favorite cake?"

"A macaron," said Edie, after another long pause.

"We're going to get along," said Good Sister June.

MAKING THE GOOD KIND OF TROUBLE

Of course, they did not get along immediately and they would not have been human if they had. Edie tried to run away from the school within days of arriving and it was only after she sat down with Good Sister June and the two of them ate patisserie together between the walls of the school[32] that Edie decided she would stay. And it was only then that she began to learn that this was not quite the school that her grandmother thought it was.

For the pupils of the School of the Good Sisters learned *useful* things.

They learned light aircraft maintenance with Good Sister Paulette; how to cater for impromptu midnight feasts with Good Sister Honey; and how to stargaze with Good Sister Robin. In between all of that, they learned how to bake sponge cakes to a recipe that never failed; how to navigate through a

....

32 I appreciate that this will sound very odd to you if you do not know my school. It is a haphazard and delightfully strange building that has been added to and taken away from over the years, and all of this has left it with hidden passageways, rooms where there should not be rooms, and a lot more towers than any building of its size should really have.

forest by working out the location of the sun and the moon; and how to build the most perfect library ever. Edie attended her lessons in disbelief at first, not quite understanding what was happening about her, and then all of a sudden she did, and she loved it. This was the sort of school that would teach her everything her parents wanted her to know and a thousand things besides. It was perfect. Within weeks she knew how to order a slice of cake in five different languages,[33] the difference between a tiramisu and a black forest gateau, and which was the best Moomin.[34]

When she met the two people who were to become her best friends, Edie loved it even more.

---

[33] Spanish: *"Por favor, ¿puedo tener un trozo de pastel?"*
Albanian: *"Ju lutem mund të bëj një fetë tortë?"*
Norwegian: *"Kan jeg ta et stykke kake?"*
Esperanto: *"Plaĉi al ĉu mi povas havi tranĉ de kuko?"*
Klingon: *"NuqDaq yuch Dapol?"*

[34] This is a trick question: The answer is "all of them."

INTRODUCING THE BEST FRIENDS

- Hanna Kowalczyk. Brown hair. Polish. Fond of books and libraries and reading. She is very passionate about letting people read what they want, when they want, and having a good bun after they're done. Her friendship with Edie began the day she arrived in the North Tower bedroom and revealed a suitcase that was more full of biscuits than useful things like socks and flannels.
- Calla North. Yellow hair. British. Fond of problem-solving, paying bills on time, and chips with far too much salt on top. She'd joined the school only the previous month and had quite the complicated first term, but all of that eventually got sorted out.[35] Her favorite cake is a white chocolate wafer, which technically isn't a cake at all, but I'll let it go just this once. Hanna and Edie hadn't expected their friendship to ever become

---

35 You can read all about it in a book called *How to Be Brave*, which was written by me as well.

a triangle, but it did when Calla arrived and it became better than they had ever imagined it could be.

And if you remember nobody else's name in this book, I would like you to remember theirs.

ENOUGH OF BISCUITS AND BACKSTORY

Good news, my dear reader. It is eleven o'clock and there is a pink wafer with my name on it. Metaphorically.[36] Whilst I eat it, I shall bring you forward to the present day in this story and tell you all about the twelve-year-old girl who showed up in Good Sister June's office and begged permission to teach a class. There was method to her madness here: The lower school was about to visit Paris on a trip, and she—as she pointed out—had some knowledge on the subject.

(I do hope you know who I am talking about, but just in case you don't, her name rhymes with "Schmedie Schmerger.")

"It is clear that the girls would *benefit* from my skills," she said brightly. "Last year, you allowed the first-years to teach synchronized swimming before we went to Venice. This was in addition to Maisie Holloway and Violet Thompson's class on chocolate pizzas and the *most* remarkable Italian opera from Grace Macdonald."

"They were accompanied by Good Sister Paulette playing

---

36 We tried labeling the biscuits once and that was . . . chaotic.

the spoons," replied Good Sister June, who had enjoyed this baffling endeavor more than she'd ever thought possible.

"Indeed," said dear Schmedie, "but my *point* is that if you're letting Ellen Beaufort turn one of the spare sheds into a cheese factory,[37] and Thea De Grazie do her talk on French music, and Eloise Taylor and Good Sister Honey make *pain au chocolat* because all of these are important and relevant for our upcoming trip to Paris, then it is only right that I lead a class of my very own."

When an argument is presented with such honest simplicity, there is very little one can do other than agree with everything it proposes. Good Sister June was no exception. "Of course," she said. "It will be a treat to have you lead a lesson. What will you be teaching us?"

"How to build a barricade," said Edie Berger. "And it will be the best lesson of all."

---

37 She was being nobly assisted in this endeavor by Good Sister Paulette, who was very talented at pulling the first-years out of the whey. This was because they were up to no gouda.

DO YOU HEAR THE SMALL GIRLS SING?

"Truth is at the heart of every good barricade," said Edie, as she studied the group of girls gathered in front of her. She felt as if she was delivering a speech before battle and the feeling was very satisfying indeed, especially because she had just watched the first-years bicker over who got to sit in the front row.[38] "A barricade also asks for stable foundations, realistic engineering, and a few points where you can stand on top of it and sing your songs of freedom. If you are protesting, then you need a barricade, for it is the heart of your protest. But! The barricade does not exist in isolation, my students; it blocks a street—yes—but we need something else for our protest to be successful. Does anybody have any suggestions?"

"Books," Hanna said with intense purpose. "I've actually been putting together a reading list for our trip to Paris. If we

....

38 For the record, Maisie Holloway won due to her having bribed Sethi Gopal to faint on cue and cause a distraction. This cost Maisie a helping of chocolate sponge and rainbow custard, several slices of rocky road, and a bag of fudge. Between you and me, I think that Sethi should charge more for her remarkable talents.

start with *Piglettes* and then move on to *Les Misérables,* we'll do SUPER well—"

"That is very helpful, my dear Hanna Banana," said Edie, who was very used to Hanna's moments of being quite heartfelt over books. "I was, however, thinking more about the paraphernalia of the protest and not the reading material we should provide our fellow protestors with."

Ellen Beaufort stuck up her hand excitedly. "Protest signs. I need a new project and we could totally start putting together some placards. You just need some thin board and a couple of broom handles, and some smart-yet-pithy slogans."

"Also wrong," said Edie, who was thoroughly enjoying being in charge in legitimate circumstances for once. "The correct answer is lunch." A dreamy look ran across her face and for a moment she forgot that she was in front of a class. Lunch was one of her most beloved things and worthy of important thought. "For a day such as this, I would take olives, of course, but also some fine fresh bread and *potentially* a little bit of tapenade."

It was only when Hanna coughed and made dramatic gestures at the room full of people around them that Edie suddenly remembered she was supposed to be teaching a class.

"So!" said Edie, giving Hanna a quick grin of thanks. "Let us imagine that you have your lunch and your urge to cause havoc! A good pairing, yes, but you must not fly into battle unprepared. As my parents would tell you, one must pause and plan and pause and plan again. You need to think about things like maximum visibility and maximum inconvenience to your enemies. You must think about where to place your barricade so that it can be seen by them and get in the most way. So, my friends, where in a school would that be?"

"The hall," said one of the first-years. "You get in the way of the meals."

Edie smiled at her like a queen blessing her subject. "You are CLEARLY destined for greatness, for this is the EXACT answer. A revolution begins where the food is. As my mother once told me, one must make friends with the cook or make enemies of them."

"But I like Good Sister Honey," said a second first-year in tragic fashion.

"It is METAPHORICAL, my little midget gem," said Edie. She leaned forward and gently patted the second first-year on the head. "Today you will build a barricade and I promise it will be the best day ever! You must choose a location within this school and protect it with your life. Or, at the very least, protect it with the life of the person you are standing next to. Anyway! Pick your materials for your barricade wisely. We have permission to use everything in the school—"

"Everything but the BOOKS," said Hanna. "If anybody hurts the library, I shall come and make ghost noises outside their window from now until the end of time."

"The library will be fine," Edie said calmingly. She climbed on top of the nearest chair and glared at the girls. "Everything in the school BUT THE BOOKS is available for you to barricade your location, but be nice to it, for we have to put it all back once we are done. You have an hour and if, by that time, I can walk past where you are without impediment—that is to say that there is nothing blocking me from doing so—I shall fail you and remind you of this failure all your life." And when nobody moved, Edie raised one fist in the air and fixed them all with a firm look. "Go! Go now! Quickly! You have a barricade to build, my friends, and it will not build itself! Deeds, not words! *Vive la révolution! Liberté, égalité, fraternité!*"

It was only when the nuns, who had been sitting at the back and quietly listening to all of this, began to grab the chairs about them and build a wall that the room burst into life. Hanna grabbed Calla's hand and pulled her toward the door. A small gaggle of first-years pushed past them and yelled, "We're going to barricade the fifth-form common room and you can't stop us!" before hurtling hysterically out of the room. Several of the elder girls opened the nearest windows and threw out ropes, preparing to rappel down the outside and barricade the front door.

And because of all of this noise and excitement, none of them saw Good Sister June and Edie exit the room in the opposite direction.

A COMPLICATED CONVERSATION

Good Sister June led Edie around the corner away from the classroom, and as the noise of the revolution began to quiet behind them, Edie gave her headmistress a look of doubt. "Was my class not good? Did I not do something correctly?"

"Your class was wonderful," said Good Sister June instantly. Although she had missed a lot of it due to the topic she was about to discuss with Edie, she had managed to see the last five minutes. It had been a remarkably empowering experience. "It felt rather like eating five cupcakes at once," she said. "I feel as if I could swim to the bottom of the world and be back in time for supper. I enjoyed every minute of it."

Edie nodded in a satisfied manner. "You know I have been working for this moment for so long. I *had* thought that once I left school I would go to run some sort of revolutionary training camp somewhere, but there may be a different option for me to now consider. I suspect I would be a Quite Good teacher. I could even teach here."

"I think you'd make a splendid teacher," said Good Sister June. The thought of a generation of girls educated by Edie Berger was something quite remarkable indeed, but then honesty compelled her to add, "But to teach here, you need to be a nun, and I'm not sure you'd make a very good one of those."

"That is true," Edie said graciously. "But this is not what you came to talk to me about."

Good Sister June had never been able to keep secrets from Edie. She had tried, of course, for that was the Appropriately Adult thing to do when one was the headmistress and the other her pupil. However, there was something about the small French girl that made that sort of thing completely impossible.

"You're right," said Good Sister June eventually. "I do have something else to talk to you about."

"Then make it quick. I suspect that those legs at the window there belong to Eloise Taylor, who, for some reason, is being dangled from her tower rather than making a barricade. Or perhaps she *is* the barricade? It is an interesting approach."

"Edie, I've had a phone call from your grandmother," said Good Sister June.

"Ah," said Edie.

THE VALUE OF EMERGENCY BISCUITS

I am sure you have come across certain words in your life that mean much more than what you intend for them to mean. For example, have you ever said yes to something while meaning *I really don't want to do it but I think I will have to deal with a lot of problems if I don't so I'll do it but under protest and I hope you never ask me to do it again?*[39]

Edie's "Ah" to Good Sister June was a very complicated thing. It said *I had forgotten about* her and *I don't want to hear what* she *has to say* and *I guess the legs of Eloise Taylor will have to wait then* and *Actually, I sort of do know what my grandmother wanted to say but I don't want to admit it* and *Why did she have to phone now in the middle of the best moment of my life?*

Luckily enough, Good Sister June had accidentally-on-purpose taken Edie to a very particular point in the school. When Edie said "Ah," Good Sister June said, "Hang on," and

....

39 Between you and me, this was precisely the response I gave Good Sister Honey when she asked me to try a kale cupcake. I was very sure it would not be a positive experience for either of us and I was quite right indeed.

then reached into the cupboard to get out a pack of biscuits. She gave Edie one and then had one herself. It was the very best thing to do under the circumstances. A well-timed biscuit can be quite the emotionally restorative act.

It was only when Edie had finished her first wafer and was starting her second that Good Sister June decided she felt confident enough to continue. "I wanted to talk to you about our trip to Paris," she said. "As you know, the entire lower school is going. That means all of the first-years, all of the seconds, and some of the older girls who are specializing in languages as well. It's basically a lot of people. And your grandmother has offered us the château to stay in rather than a hotel."

"Ah," said Edie again, in quite a different tone of voice. This time her "Ah" meant: *Why has she offered to do that?* and *My grand-mère hasn't talked to me for years* and *My parents can't stand her* and *I think I might actually feel a little bit sick.*

Good Sister June gave her another emergency biscuit.

Edie broke it in two and gave half of it back.

Once they had finished eating, Edie took a deep breath. "Did you accept?"

"No," said Good Sister June. "I told her that I was grateful—and I am. Staying in the château will save us a *lot* of money, but I needed to talk it over with you first."

"I do not want to talk about this," said Edie.

"That's all right."

"I do not want to talk about *her*," said Edie.

"I'm sorry," said Good Sister June.

"I am not crying," said Edie.

"I know," said Good Sister June.

THE FLOWER-PURCHASING HABITS[40] OF SOEUR CHANTAL

Not Crying is when you want to cry your eyes out but also don't want to cry one bit. I would recommend that you have to hand an emergency biscuit because it is precisely the sort of emergency that requires a very good biscuit.

Just in case you don't have a very good biscuit,[41] I shall also give you some advice. When you need to Not Cry, you should try to stay as still as you can and ignore everything that's going on around you. The world may be moving a thousand miles in all directions, but when you are Not Crying you are quite allowed to ignore it. All you need to do is stand very still and take a deep breath and count to ten. If you do not know how to count to ten, then count however far you know and just keep going.

Once I got to 317 but that, my friends, is a different story.

....

40 A pun! Nuns wear habits and have habits, and so this chapter heading is rather a good pun and I am most proud of it.

41 You really should have an emergency biscuit stash in your house. A sock drawer would be ideal. You must, however, make sure that the socks are clean and the biscuits are wrapped. There is no joy to be found in a crumbly sock drawer.

In this story, Good Sister June saw the signs of a Not Cry and reacted in the best and only way.

She gave Edie another biscuit.

"Count to ten," said Good Sister June, "and while you're doing that, let me tell you what else your grandmother said. Or rather, what she did not say. Technically she hasn't told me anything, of course, but I rather think that your grandmother has been experiencing some problems recently. Sœur[42] Chantal from the Paris convent goes to your mother's plant shop and the lady who works there heard something from the cleaner at the château."

Edie looked at Good Sister June out of the corner of her eye. A little flicker of interest began to burn inside her heart.

"Somebody has been trying to steal something from the château," said Good Sister June, who was in the process of helping herself to her own emergency biscuit. She turned back to Edie. "They keep heading to the same room every time on the ground floor. It's like they're after a specific something."

"It must be one of the paintings from the collection," said Edie. "There are so many priceless things in there for them to choose from. It would not be the first time somebody has targeted it. Somebody broke in before but I scared him off. Also, I gave a remarkably accurate description to the police but they never found out who he was. Maybe he has begun to try again."

"How strange," said Good Sister June softly, trying to work

---

42 This is French for "Sister," and I know it looks a bit strange but just pronounce it like *sir* and all will be well.

it all out inside her head. "If it's causing your grandmother so much trouble, I wonder why she hasn't sent any of the collection away? She could donate the paintings to a museum or put them into storage somewhere safe, I imagine. It must be scary. Alone in that big house and knowing that somebody is trying to break in and take something very precious away from you. She clearly cares about it an awful lot."

"Perhaps she should send it to England like she does with everything else she supposedly cares so much about."

Good Sister June gave Edie a *Come On, You're Better Than That* look. "Perhaps she might benefit from a collection of nuns with remarkable self-defense skills. Good Sister Robin is very talented in jiujitsu, and Good Sister Gwendolyn is really very knowledgeable on poison darts. Under any other circumstances, I would be concerned for the girls' welfare, but when presented with such remarkable staff as ours, I do not think that is an issue. I'd be happy for us to stay there and help her to feel safer in her home, but only if you wished it. There are other hotels in Paris for us to look at."

"You don't have to look at the others. You can stay at the château."

"We can what?" said Good Sister June, unable to stop herself.

"Stay at the château," said Edie. "I'm giving you my permission."

"You know you don't have to."

"But I do, I do," said Edie. "I really do."

IN THE NORTH TOWER BEDROOM

Whilst all of this had been happening, Calla North and Hanna Kowalczyk had been busily barricading the entrance to the North Tower bedroom. The North Tower is a completely round room, accessible by a long flight of stairs from the entry hall, and on a normal day it contains three beds and three small girls. The three girls are Calla, Hanna, and Edie, and sometimes the three of them spend more time on the roof just outside of the bedroom and sometimes they have midnight feasts in one of the other towers, but I am assured that they definitely do sleep in their beds.

At least, occasionally.

Calla's side of the room is the tidiest. She has lived a life where she does not have many things to tidy and look after and so the few things that she has are neat and in order. Her most important possession is a satellite phone that connects to her mother, Elizabeth, wherever she is in the world. After Elizabeth's last expedition,[43] Good Sister Paulette had hacked

---

43   Elizabeth North is a researcher of ducks. She is the best at it in the entire world, and now at last, the world has learned what an important and remarkable skill this is. For a long time it did not, but that is another story.

her satellite phone to emit a constant GPS signal to an app on Calla's mobile. Calla had been doubtful that this would work (for her mother was not gifted with practical skills) but so far, it had done just fine. She had tracked the little red dot as it moved steadily through the Andes, and every time she looked at it she knew that on the other side of it was her mother, and she was well.

Hanna's side of the room is more book than person. Technically there is a bed in the middle of it, but in truth she sleeps amid piles of books and carefully placed emergency biscuits. This is her library and she picks titles for her fellow readers at school and storybooks to read out loud to the innumerable first-years who beg her for such things on a regular basis. Of course, she also sometimes just sits and stares at all of her books and strokes their spines in a soft and happy manner.[44]

Edie's side of the room is different again. Her bed is almost invisible under the amount of pillows and clothes she has piled on top of it. Whenever she goes to sleep, she simply burrows underneath all of this and curls around the socks and T-shirts that she has left there. Ultimately, if I am honest, she ends up providing a rather convincing impression of a polar bear going into hibernation for the winter. Her walls are covered with posters of revolutionary heroes that she bought online: posters of Che Guevara,[45]

....

44 She is currently reading *The Railway Children* by E. Nesbit and has asked me to tell you that it is very good, but you will cry a lot at the end of it.

45 Ernesto "Che" Guevara (June 14, 1928–October 9, 1967) was a vital figure of the Cuban revolution, and somebody who looked very dashing in photographs.

Rosa Luxembourg,[46] and Toussaint Louverture[47] among many others. There is a very small framed picture at the side of her bed of her mother and father, and sometimes I think that is the most important thing of all.

The middle of the room is a communal area, where the three girls meet to do their homework and to divide out the cake that Good Sister Honey so kindly provides for midnight feasts. Once they finished building their barricade, Calla and Hanna decided to celebrate with a substantial slice of red velvet cake. Their main topic of discussion was the absence of Edie herself.

"She *has* been gone a long time," said Hanna, as she thoughtfully divided the sponge from the icing so that she could eat the best part last.[48] "Maybe she's gotten stuck in the barricade that the first-years were building. The last thing I saw, they were winching a desk up the side of the building and Heather Kirk was sitting on top of it."

"That's not a barricade," said Calla, as she helped herself to Hanna's sponge. "Actually, I think it's more of a weird attempt at making a lift?"

....

46 Rosa Luxemburg (March 5, 1871–January 15, 1919) was a philosopher and thinker, and believed very much in the power of the masses to rise up and lead revolutions. She was one of Edie's very favorite people, even though she did not agree with everything she said or did. But then, as Edie would tell you herself, disagreeable people are all the more interesting because of that.

47 Toussaint Louverture (20 May 1743–7 April 1803) was a hero of the Haitian revolution and helped ensure the end of colonialism and slavery on the island, which makes him a very excellent chap indeed.

48 The best part of any cake is the icing. Any other opinion on this is deeply, utterly wrong.

"Which is why I marked them down for it," said Edie herself as she climbed in through the open window from the roof. "The desk never got to the top and Heather Kirk is now being rescued by Good Sister Christine and her rappelling equipment, which, between you and me, is less 'revolution' and more 'slightly embarrassing predicament.'" When Edie was fully inside, she walked over to the barricade at the door and wrinkled her nose with disappointment. "Alas, I'm going to have to mark you two down as well. Anybody could have come in the way I did and stolen all of your emergency biscuits. I thought I had taught you both better than that. It is like you have not attended *any* of my midnight lectures on revolutionary techniques."

"Enough of that," said Hanna, who clearly had her priorities in order. "Do you want some cake?"

"I do not want cake," said Edie.

"Oh my god," said Hanna. "Are you *ill*?"

"I am *fine*," said Edie. "Sit *down*, Calla, you do not need to call the nurse on me."[49]

Calla sat. She studied Edie for a long moment and then, in a very tactful and gentle voice, she said, "Do you want to tell us what's wrong?" It was quite obvious that there *was* something the matter. She had never seen Edie refuse cake. It was practically apocalyptic.

"My grand-mère has offered the château for the school to stay in while we are in Paris," said Edie.

---

49 I know that was a lot of italics in a short amount of time, but it was the only way to give you an idea of the *very pointed* conversation that Edie and Hanna were having.

"And that's a problem because?" said Calla.

"Because Edie and her grand-mère never talk," said Hanna, putting down her cake fork.[50] "I mean, I know your parents can't stay in touch easily, Edie, because of all the traveling they do, but she's got no excuse. All she needed to do was phone you every now and then and make things a little less weird than what they are."

"Well, she phoned Good Sister June," replied Edie, even though she did not want to. "She offered the château for our trip and Good Sister June came to ask me if it was all right. She also told me that somebody keeps breaking into the château. Of course, I have already stopped a thief before from doing such a thing and I am quite capable of stopping another. So! We shall go, we will stay at my family's château, we will figure out who this new thief is and stop them, and you two can make sure that I spend no time with my grand-mère whatsoever."

And as she finished, Edie realized that she was exhausted in a way that she had never been before. She walked over to her bed and got in, pausing only to take her shoes off. She pulled the blanket over her head, and then for good measure put the pillow there as well.

"Wow," said Calla.

"I don't know what to say to *any* of that," said Hanna.

"Well," said Edie's pillow. "That makes three of us."

---

50 An apocalyptic act in itself.

WHAT TO DO AFTER AN
AWKWARD SILENCE

Edie stayed under that pillow and blanket for two days and nights and only surfaced on the morning that the school was due to depart for Paris. The wider school thought that she was unwell, and in a way, they were not wrong. Edie was used to living her life with a determination that could make grown men weep, and the thought of seeing her grandmother and being back at the château had made her heart break into a thousand different pieces. One of those pieces was scared, another was angry, and another still was nervous of what would happen when the two of them met for the first time in several years.[51] She did not tell anybody any of this, and the Good Sisters did not ask it of her. Instead they brought her food and drink and took turns to sit quietly with her until one day when Good Sister June was there, and Edie reached out from under her blanket and squeezed her hand.

....

[51] Although there had been opportunities for Edie to go home—for things like the summer holidays and Christmas—she had not. She had stayed at the school with Hanna and the other girls whose families were away. She could have gone back to the château, but she did not want to. Something very sad inside her heart had stopped her every time.

"She sent me here as a punishment," said Edie softly. She had thought about everything that had happened since her parents had left her with Odette, and this had been the one moment that she kept coming back to. The way that her grandmother had sent her away from the only home she'd ever known. The way she'd taken everything away from her.

"I know," said Good Sister June. "I have often wondered what she actually meant by that."

"What are you going to tell her?"

"I don't know," said Good Sister June. She squeezed Edie's hand back. "I won't tell her that you're a bad young lady, if that's what you're worried about. I don't think anybody really is bad. Everybody has choices to make and it's what they do with them that matters. Last term, for example, you chose to help somebody who needed your help very much. That tells me a lot about the sort of person that you are."

"She won't understand that, though," said Edie.

"Perhaps she's not the one who needs to understand it," said Good Sister June.

NEVER TRAVEL WITHOUT A FLANNEL

On the morning of the trip itself, Edie was the first to wake. She had been dreaming of the shops on the Rue de la Vérité and for a moment it was as if she had been there all along, watching Madame Laurentis put handmade chocolates into her shop window and Frau Bettelstein sprinkle caraway seeds onto her fluffy pillows of dough. It was only when Hanna let out a surprisingly loud snore and Calla whispered something in her sleep that Edie realized that she was still at school.

But not for long, she told herself, because today was *the* day. She was going home. She was going back to Paris and to the château and to her friends on the Rue de la Vérité. And although a big part of her was terrified and another big part of her was sad, an even bigger part was excited about going back to somewhere that was so full of her parents. She didn't think of them in England. She'd tried, but it just didn't work. Paris, on the other hand, had them in every inch of it. Her mother organizing a protest on the street corner. Her father quietly arguing his case against people who didn't believe him. The three of them eating breakfast on the bench at the end of the Rue de la Vérité, together.

All of the memories that she thought she'd forgotten, suddenly as fresh and bright as the day that they were first made.

Edie took a deep breath and bounced out of bed. She dressed quickly, before tiptoeing over to where Calla and Hanna were asleep, and then, because even though she was experiencing some Substantial Feelings, she was still Edie Berger, and she bellowed: "WAKE UP!"

Calla said something Quite Rude.[52]

Hanna said something Even Ruder.[53]

Edie gave them both a benevolent smile. "Today is the day we go to Paris and you are NOT PACKED. You *know* that we have to be downstairs on time, and you *know* that Good Sister Christine is going to come in soon and ask you why you have not packed an extra flannel, and you *know* that I am just trying to help you deal with all of that."

"But I haven't even picked my books yet," said Hanna. "I've narrowed them down to *The Little Princess* and *The Secret Garden* and *Charlotte's Web* and I can't narrow them down any more."

"Well, you must," said Good Sister Christine as she swept into the North Tower bedroom. I am not sure if you have ever witnessed a nun walking into your bedroom, so let me tell you that it is quite the dramatic moment. It is a little like having a human-sized penguin come to join you. "I have been sent to check on your packing and here you are, clearly not packed."

"My BOOKS," said Hanna plaintively.

---

52 "COLD CUSTARD!"
53 "CHOCOLATE CAKE FILLED WITH JAM!"

"You'll have to leave one behind," Good Sister Christine said with the confidence of somebody who had already packed ten books[54] in her own suitcase and another one in her travel bag for luck. And then, because she was human and could not stop herself, she added: "Maybe two."

"I can't," Hanna said tragically.

"You must," said Good Sister Christine. "I need you all on the bus in fifteen minutes, or we are going to go without you." She glanced around the room. There were many bedrooms at the School of the Good Sisters but this was the one she loved the most. Sometimes, however, it took a moment for her to quite remember why. This was one of those moments. Calla was texting her mother[55] with one hand and trying to put on her socks with the other. Hanna was surrounded by books and very little else. Edie was the only one who had gotten dressed and had packed her bag. Good Sister Christine smiled. "Are you ready?"

"Yes," said Edie slowly, "I think I am."

....

54 Good Sister Christine's book selection included: *Zen and the Art of Wimple Maintenance*; *Catch-22 Habits*; and *A Tale of Two Flannels*. She assures me that they are all very good.

55 It may interest you to know that Good Sister Christine and Calla's mum, Elizabeth, were best friends from their own school days. Calla often had to pass messages on from the nun to Elizabeth. She had attempted to teach Good Sister Christine how to text herself but that was like attempting to make kale a pleasant and passable ingredient in anything. Impossible.

DO NOT FALL OFF THE BOAT

They arrived at the port much sooner than Edie thought they would. A part of her had become so used to living in England and in the middle of nowhere, surrounded by nuns and girls and sugary confections, she had forgotten how close they were to everything else. When the bus queued up at the port in a line of coaches and vans, and another line of trucks began to line up next to them, her heart started to beat with excitement. She was going home, and even though her grandmother was going to be there, there would be a thousand other people to see. Herr and Frau Bettelstein. Madame Laurentis. Isabelle Tremont, who was looking after the plant shop.

"Calla," Edie said, poking her gently in the ribs. "I am quite excited about this trip. I have not wanted to go home for a long time, but I think I do now."

It was a little like the day before one of her parents' demonstrations, she thought. Her whole stomach was full of butterflies and doubt, but underneath it all was excitement. She couldn't wait for what was about to happen.

"Me too," said Calla, who hadn't been out of the country in her entire life. Her eyes were big and wide as she took it all in. "I mean, how can you not be excited about this?" She was still making little squeaks of astonishment at everything thirty minutes later, once all eighty-six students and twelve nuns had been herded onto the ferry,[56] Good Sister Gwendolyn had been rescued from the temptations of the Duty-Free, and Hanna had been persuaded to leave her books on the bus all by themselves for a few hours.

It was at this point that Good Sister June shared some useful and brief words of advice. "Do not fall off. Nuns do not swim unless the temperature is of a balmy and tropical nature and we have been plied with cocktails beforehand. The English Channel is neither balmy nor tropical so if you do fall off, you need to make sure you can get back on without our help. When the ship arrives at Calais, they will make an announcement to tell everybody to get ready to get off. When you hear that, I expect to see you all here and then we'll get back on the bus. If you are not here and we have to go looking for you, then I will make sure you eat kale for the entire trip."[57]

The girls nodded their agreement before scattering all over the ferry. Several first-years got stuck in the lift, another set of first-years couldn't find the stairs and instead decided to rappel from the sunshine deck to the staff quarters, and another group entirely found themselves in the restaurant's

---

[56] Good Sister Robin was not gifted with a sense of direction, let me tell you that for free.

[57] I would like to say that this punishment had not been applied to Good Sister June in her own childhood, but that would be a lie.

kitchen and decided to help them cook lunch.[58] Good Sister Gwendolyn took her covert-skills class over to the lifeboats for a lecture on how to survive in the middle of the sea,[59] while Hanna and Calla and Edie went straight up to the top deck and found a bench that was at the front of the boat. Hanna produced biscuits out of one of her pockets, and handed them round. "Every journey deserves biscuits," she said in the wise way that makes her one of my favorite people in the entire world. "Calla, you should have two because you're looking quite overwhelmed by everything, and you, Edie, should have one because there are things we need to know about your granny, and we need to know them now."

"All right," said Edie. "Then we shall begin."

---

58 "It's not that I wish to say you're doing anything wrong," said a very earnest Lucy Millais to a quite confused chef, "but I think you've overwhipped your meringue."

59 Carefully.

THIS IS WHERE YOU BEGIN

"My friends, there are two types of trouble," said Edie. "One of them is the bad sort of trouble, the sort that you should not ever do, and then there is the good sort of trouble. My family, we are known for the good sort of trouble, and we are proud of it. We have been known for it as long as I can remember. For forever, I think. Anyway! An example: I have an ancestor who helped people escape the French Revolution.[60] Another was a hero in World War One who sheltered refugees in the attics of the château.[61] Also my great-great-aunt was a pirate who robbed from the rich and gave to the poor—"

. . . .

60 Hortense Adelaide Berger, a tiny and quite beautiful woman. She was possessed of a dazzling bravery and confidence that allowed her to walk into the homes of people who were under threat from the revolutionaries, and walk out with them at her side. The secret was to never blink, she told them.

61 Jacqueline Anais Berger, who, whilst out one day, had thought that the Seine had burst its banks and had flooded the side streets. But when she got closer, she had realized that the dark water was just people with nowhere to go, thousands of refugees all packed tightly together, and with a bravery that dazzles me even now, she had given as many of them as she could a home. Sometimes when I do not know what to do I think about what Jacqueline would do under the circumstances, and I know I shall not go wrong.

"I'm sure that's Robin Hood," said Hanna.

Edie held up a hand. "He had a French soul and that is what counts," she said. "But! Do not distract me, Hanna, my little cabbage, for I am telling you about my family and how we do the things that other people do not know how to do. My maman, she learned these skills from the lady who owned her shop, and when she met my papa, it was love at first sight between them. But then she had to meet his grand-mère and *she* had spent her life trying to stop my papa from living up to his destiny—even sending him to a school in England.[62] She could not, however, stop him from falling in love with somebody who was just as brave and revolutionary as he was. She did not like it, but she could not stop it. So! The moment I was old enough to fend for myself, they left me with her and went off to save the world. They did not come back—then, or ever—and *she* hated it. And me. I am the embodiment of everything she detests."[63]

"I'm sure that's not true," said Calla, who hadn't ever had a grandparent in her life to think about, let alone one to think about like this. The whole conversation mystified her in a way she could not quite understand.

"But it *is*," said Edie. "I mean, do not get me wrong. I am

....

62 Does this sound familiar? It should.

63 It is important for me to tell you at this point that Edie is the embodiment of everything good and true in the world, and it breaks my heart that she felt like this. When she told me what she said to the other two (for she very much wanted me to get this chapter right), I waited until she had finished and then gave her a big hug. Also a slice of swiss roll. They were given one after the other, just to clarify. If they had been given at the same time, I do not think it would have been a pleasant experience.

so excited to go home and show you everything in my city and introduce you to your first-ever proper croissant, but *she* will be there and I do not think that she will have changed. Even though we have not talked for years, I know that much at least."

"So why does she want to talk to you now?" said Calla.

Edie took a deep breath to answer and then stopped as a quite-curious thought hit her: She did not know. She had spent years knowing everything about her own life. Jean-Claude and Marianne had shared every decision that they could with her. Quite often the three of them would sit in the shop as the sun set and argue out the problem between them and try to figure out what they should do. Even though she was a child, her opinion had mattered. Her parents had looked for it and wanted it, and then all of a sudden her grand-mère had not.

"I do not know," said Edie eventually.

"Maybe it's like *The Little Princess* and you're secretly the heiress to some diamond mines and she's calling you back to tell you," said Hanna, clutching the vague memory of one of the more dramatic stories she'd read. "Oh! Or maybe it's like *Bride Leads the Chalet School* and you've got to return to Paris to become a sheep farmer."

"I thank you for your thoughts, my dear Hanna Banana, as chaotic and as incompressible as they are," said Edie with all the tact she could muster. "And if my grand-mère does present me with a sheep, then you will be the first to know. However, there is another more pressing manner. One of the first-years has just swan-dived into the ocean, and I imagine we should go and fish her out of it."

COMING HOME

Once all of the first-years had been rescued and a brief award ceremony had been held for the best diver,[64] Edie, Hanna, and Calla went inside. They found Good Sister Honey, who offered them a chocolate spread sandwich each (an offer that they accepted most happily) before finding somewhere else to sit. For a while, none of them spoke. They were too happy eating and staring out the window at the sea. They had seen water before, but it had never looked like this. This was light and dark and shadow and shade. This was blue and green and black and gray. This was deeper, too, than they'd ever thought it could be. It was a little bit scary and a little bit lovely, all at once.

Edie couldn't take her eyes off it. The last time she had crossed the channel had been all by herself, in a train in a dark and dull tunnel far underneath the sea.

Boats were so much better.

....

64 Maisie Holloway won for her remarkable reverse dive with three somersaults in the pike position, and also because she managed to tie Jia Liu's shoes together as she went past her.

And boats with her best friends at her side were the Best Sort of Better.

As Edie studied the view, an outline began to appear in the distance. She wasn't sure what it was at first, but she knew it was something important. A dark cloud, maybe, or somewhere the color and the light and the air just seemed to be a little bit more solid than before. She had never seen anything like it, and for a long moment, she simply stared at the magical thing before she realized that it was a whole new country coming into view, and that country was her home.

She was back, she was back.

MEET THE FAMILY

After an hour or two of countryside and long, bland fields, they arrived in Paris, and Edie could not take her eyes off it. The bus drove past tall houses and high-rises and down onto a wide road where the traffic was faster than she had ever remembered it to be. She found herself constantly holding her breath, convinced that they'd all be crashing into each other in moments, and then, when it didn't happen, she blew out onto the window and drew a little heart into the fog and the glass. She had forgotten the way her city *felt*. Every inch of it burned with life and excitement, and being in the middle of it again, even with the promise of seeing her grandmother shortly, was one of the best feelings she had ever had.

Calla leaned over her at one point and stared out of the window. "Everything's the same and yet actually a bit different." She hadn't stopped staring at it all since they had gotten off the boat that morning.

"I think what you mean is *better*," said Edie with some satisfaction. "*Everything* French is better. Come on. Test me. Sausages? Better. Cheese? Better. PUDDINGS? Much better."

The moment that she finished speaking, Hanna poked her

head through the gap in the seat behind them. I think she was going to reply to this remarkable litany from Edie but was distracted when the small French girl booped her gently on the nose.[65] "Hanna, what are you doing here? Are you also on a school trip? Such a coincidence! A part of me thought you might still be at school, counting your books and telling them how much you love them. By the way, how many books *did* you bring?"

Hanna gave her a severe look. "Not enough,"[66] she said. "Oh, *look*, it's the River Seine. My parents came here on a diplomatic mission once, and they had to find somebody who was hiding from them down by the side of it. I wonder if it was this bit or farther down. I mean, they said it wasn't the best place to hide because there's really nowhere *to* hide by a river unless you're under a bridge or, you know, under the actual water."

"What are you talking about?" said Edie. She gave Calla a quick glance, wondering if she was going to join in, but she was quite busy making a *Did She Just Say What I Thought She Said?* face.

"Diplomacy can be very complicated," said Hanna, as if that

....

65 Just in case you found that word as confusing as I did, I had to check what *booping* means with Edie. She tells me that it is gently yet affectionately tapping somebody that you are close to. I recommend not doing it with strangers. Or unprepared nuns. I am still recovering from Edie's remarkable practical demonstration.

66 Hanna packed seventeen books, five packets of custard creams, and precisely zero flannels. She was not looking forward to the moment when Good Sister Christine realized this.

all made sense, and then changing the subject, she cried, "Look! Everyone look out the window!" and there was the Eiffel Tower in all her glory, stretching high above the city. "It is three hundred and twenty-four meters and weighs just over ten thousand tons,"[67] said Hanna, reading from her book in a voice that the whole bus could hear.[68] "It's the same height as an eighty-one-story building. A story is one whole floor of a building, so that's pretty big. And did you know that the tower can shrink several inches during cold weather because of the iron contracting, and that every film in Paris *legally*[69] has to feature it in some way so that you *know* that it's Paris without having to think too much, which makes sense because it is the most-visited monument that you have to pay to see in the entire world. I mean, you don't have to pay to see it; you have to pay to go on it."

She continued on this topic for quite some time, but Edie was Not Listening. She was too busy remembering the way it felt to stand at the top of the tower and see the city laid before her like food on a table. Jean-Claude would point out the areas and sights for her, moving his hand across the sky like a painter working on a canvas: "Montparnasse, the Arc de Triomphe, Centre Pompidou," and Marianne would nod and add a commentary of her own after each one: "Excellent

---

67 Calla, thoughtfully: "I wonder how many ducks that is." Because I am a helpful author, I have asked Good Sister Christine to work this out and she says that the Eiffel Tower weighs just under seven million ducks or, in a much more useful metric, roughly nine million Victoria sponges.

68 And, I suspect, at a volume that people back in England could still hear.

69 Calla, faintly: "I don't think this is *actually* true."

market. You must try the bread near there. Amazing community groups." And when they were all finished, they would find the slender path that was the Rue de la Vérité and wave hello to all their friends so far down below.

It was like they were driving through her memories. Every inch of the city reminded her of something she thought she'd forgotten. She stared out the window as the bus rolled past places where they'd demonstrated against climate change and signposts that still wore the faint threads of the feminist yarn-bombing that her mother had done all those years ago.

At one point Calla poked her gently in the side. "Are we there yet? Because we have been driving through Paris for days . . ."

"It's literally just been an hour since we got here," said Hanna, her head still squashed between the seats. Somehow she had managed to produce a new guidebook from somewhere and brandished it at her two friends. "Look, if you'd just *read* then you'd know more. For example, do you know what an *arrondissement* is?"[70]

Edie gave her a little grin. "I *did* grow up here."

"Sometimes I forget that," said Hanna.

"It's okay," said Edie. "I think I forgot it myself a little bit."

. . . .

70 This is the French word for a local district. There are twenty arrondissements in Paris. There are also twenty biscuits in this packet that I am eating, and bearing in mind that I'm on biscuit nineteen, I need to end this footnote here and go get some more.

HOMECOMING

After a while, the bus turned off the busy roads in the heart of Paris and started to head through the backstreets. Everything grew smaller and tighter about it until they drove up to an ornate set of gates and Good Sister Christine got out to ring a bell. Edie watched her talk to somebody through the intercom before the gates swung open and she got back on the bus.

And as they drove through the gates, Edie's stomach performed the most remarkable somersault. It was not an *I am about to be sick* somersault nor an *I have not eaten for all of twenty minutes and need an emergency biscuit to save me from starvation*, but rather an *I am experiencing a lot of emotions and do not know quite how to handle them* somersault.

"Edie," said Calla, "you look like you're experiencing a lot of emotions and do not know quite how to handle them."

"Because we are at the château and I am about to see my grand-mère for the first time in a very long time."

Calla gave her a blank look. "But we can't be at the château. There's literally nothing here but fields. I haven't been in Paris very long—or actually, ever—but I don't think it's got fields in the middle of it. No city has fields in the middle of it."

Edie pulled her knees up to her chest and stared determinedly at the back of the seat in front of her. She took a deep breath and told herself that she could handle whatever was going to happen. "They are not fields. We are driving through the gardens of the château. The estate starts at the gate we just drove through."

"Gardens," said Calla disbelievingly. "Like, more than one?" She never said much about what her life had been like before the school and before her mum's new job, but every now and then she let the odd detail out. Food banks. Bills that couldn't be paid. It had clearly been the absolute opposite of Edie's childhood in this rich and open space, and the closer they got to the château, the more Edie realized it.

"There are three gardens if you count the courtyard behind the house," Edie said very slowly. "There's a path through it down to the Rue de la Vérité. We used to walk up it every Sunday to visit my grand-mère for lunch. She kept making me eat kale."

Hanna gasped. "We'll *never* leave you alone with her." At least, I think she gasped. She was rather too squished between the seats for me to be definitive on this matter. "Kale soup is the food of an absolute monster."

And there is very little I can add to that, so I won't.

INTRODUCING ODETTE BERGER

The bus turned a final corner and all of a sudden, the Château Berger lay before it. Everybody on the bus let out a gasp at the same time and pressed themselves to the window. They had never seen anywhere as big as this building before in their lives. Several of the first-years fainted from excitement; Good Sister Robin broke into song for some reason; and Hanna and Calla stared at Edie. "You never said it was like this. You lived in a *castle*."

Edie did not answer. She was too busy watching a small and very birdlike woman walk out of the front door of the château. The woman was enormously old and yet she did not look it. She moved quickly and sharply, and the only thing that betrayed her age was the long silver cane she held in her hand to steady her when she needed it. The cane was the same color as her hair; the sort of sharp, still silver that came only in winter. She had been sitting by the window for the past two hours, dozing on and off as she waited for the bus to arrive. I wish I could tell you what she felt as she sat there, but the truth is I do not think even she knew. And so she had dozed and waited and dozed and waited, with her three small and sleepy dogs[71] and her pet duck[72] standing at her side. It was only thanks to the duck's gentle quack that Odette had woken up in time to see the bus coming at all.

As she stood there at the door, she scanned the crowd in front of her. She was looking for one girl in particular and even though the nuns spoke to her and thanked her for having them, and the first-years curtseyed in an overwhelmed and slightly confused fashion,[73] she did not hear or see any of it. She was looking for her granddaughter, and when the bus emptied and she still did not see her, a most curious expression passed across her face. It was the expression somebody might have when they looked for a chocolate cake and were presented, alas, with kale soup.

It was only the quick movement of one of her dogs and the sharp, sudden interest of the duck that made her look at the last girl getting off the bus. The girl was taller than her granddaughter was, and as Odette watched her, she walked over to talk to two other girls, one with bright yellow hair and one clutching a book to her heart. For a moment Odette could not figure out why her dogs and the duck were looking at the child and then, all of a sudden, it hit her. This girl was Edmée, and she was home.

....

71 The dogs were Sir Indigo, Countess Ginevera, and Baron Arturo, and Odette had gotten them to help guard the château after the first attempted break-in.

72 The duck's name was Henri, and Odette had gotten him after the second attempted break-in when the pet shop had run out of guard dogs but still had a guard duck left in stock.

73 Maisie Holloway was convinced that was what you did in front of elderly people. Lucy Millais's counterargument of "Yes, but only if they're from the 1800s," did not, alas, convince her otherwise.

OPENING NIGHT

Once everybody had picked up their bags, and several of the first-years had been persuaded to pick the bag that they had actually packed instead of the one that caught their eye the most, the school lined up in front of Odette and the château. Edie and Hanna and Calla were accidentally-on-purpose at the back of the group, with Edie hidden behind two of the tallest girls[74] in the school for good measure.

"You are all very welcome," said Odette, leaning slightly on her cane to support herself and trying to ignore the fact that several of the first-years had begun to have a picnic on the front lawn. "We are in the most beautiful city in the world and I am very happy that you are here and in my home.[75] Tonight,

---

74 Greta Dunn, who was destined to be a legend on the basketball field, and her twin sister, Stine, who was destined to be a legend in painting and decorating. Stine could plaster an entire room before you or I would have even picked up a paintbrush, whilst Greta can slam-dunk with one hand tied behind her back. I am not completely sure what slam dunks and plastering are, so I am trusting Stine and Greta both here and hoping that this footnote all makes some sense.

75 She was not, but not for the reasons that you may think. You'll find out why in a little while.

you must eat, and then you must sleep and make yourselves at home. My staff will show you all where to go—please follow them. I only ask that I speak to my granddaughter privately before she goes upstairs. Edmée? I don't see you. Where are you?"

Good Sister Christine gave Odette a friendly smile. "I'll find her," she said, nobly ignoring the fact that she knew exactly where Edie was. Not only was Calla's hair bright enough to find in the middle of the night, Hanna was always carrying a pile of books in her hands, and Edie was always somewhere nearby.

It was because of this that Good Sister Christine walked right over to where Edie was hiding. She spoke to Hanna and Calla first. "Go on inside. Take Edie's bag with you. You're sleeping in a room next to her bedroom. It was too small to put you all in together. One of the Good Sisters will show you where it is. Off you go."

When Calla and Hanna slowly went inside the house, Good Sister Christine turned to where Edie was standing. She said, "Your grandmother wants to talk to you." She smiled encouragingly. "I know that you're not looking forward to it, but it's better to just get this sort of thing over and done with."

"Perhaps I do not want to," said Edie, not moving an inch.

"You're not going to stay out here all night."

"I could."

"Good Sister Honey is making profiteroles for supper," said Good Sister Christine. "And I think she's going to make some hot chocolate sauce to go with them."

Edie let out a small, painful groan.

"Sorry," said Good Sister Christine.

"As you should be," said Edie. "If I must talk with *her*, I would like you to promise me one thing."

"Anything," said Good Sister Christine. "Providing that it's legal, of course."[76]

"I would like a double helping of profiteroles."

"Done."

"And I would like breakfast tomorrow to be scrambled eggs on buttery toast."

"Done and doner," said Good Sister Christine, who was very fond of both Edie and Good Sister Honey's scrambled eggs on buttery toast.

"Thank you," said Edie.

She took a deep breath.

"Do you want me to come with you?" said Good Sister Christine.

"Yes," said Edie, and then she corrected herself. Her parents had never needed anybody to hold their hands and so she wouldn't. "No. I will be all right by myself."

And then she said it again, as though to convince herself.

"I will be all right by myself."

---

76 Always a useful thing to mention to Edie Berger.

HOW TO BE BRAVE

For the first time in years, Edie walked up toward the building that she had once called home. Every step she took felt a little bit like a dream, but she kept telling herself that it was real and that she wasn't alone. Calla and Hanna were just inside, waiting for her. Good Sister June had packed emergency macarons for a midnight snack. The plant shop on the Rue de la Vérité was just a short walk away. There were profiteroles to have for supper.

She could do this.

Even if she really did not want to.

And so she ignored the first-years who couldn't remember which bag was theirs and, instead of calmly working this out, had instead decided to perform an impromptu musical, and she headed straight up to where the tiny figure of Odette Berger stood waiting for her.

"Hello, Grand-Mère," said Edie.

Odette gave her a look. It was the sort of look that only a very small and quite ferocious woman can give people who displease her and it had proven most effective in the past.

But those people were not Edie.

Who promptly gave the exact same look right back to her.

IN WHICH THINGS START TO GO HORRIBLY WRONG

"It's good to see you, Edmée," said Odette.

Edie made a small and very French noise in reply.

"How are you?" said Odette, ignoring this. She still hadn't moved. If anything, her position had become more fixed. One hand had tightened around her cane and the other rested on her hip, tightly frozen in place. "It's been years since I saw you, Edmée. You look well. I did not recognize you at first."

"My name's Edie," said Edie eventually. "Nobody calls me Edmée."

"No, it's not," said Odette. "I haven't forgotten that much."

Edie took a deep breath. "You have not *remembered* and that is quite different," she said, and it must be emphasized that she did this as tactfully as she could, which was not actually very tactful at all. "My parents have always called me Edie. You are the only one who has ever called me Edmée. Even the English call me Edie, and they are literally *awful* at saying names. And also cooking. Did I ever tell you how obsessed with sponge puddings they are? Everything is sponge. Even sponges in the bathroom, which is *so* strange to me."

"Your name is Edmée," said Odette.

"No," said Edie, rapidly giving up on tact. She had forgotten how much it did not work with her grandmother. "It is not Edmée. Not now. Nobody calls me that. Like I said, you are the only one who ever did."

"That is because it is your name," said Odette. "And please don't contradict me again. I do not like this new attitude of yours. It is giving me a headache. As are your friends. Are they always this noisy?" She paused as a particularly overexcited first-year raced past them, picked up the bag she had forgotten, whispered something apologetically at Odette,[77] and then ran back into the château.

Odette made a *That's Exactly My Point* face.

"You do not know them," said Edie.

"I am not sure I want to."

"You are not being fair," said Edie, studying her grandmother as though she was a scientific experiment. "I admit that the first-years are noisy and somewhat incomprehensible at times, and I *also* admit that the big girls would not know a good baguette if it hit them on the nose, and a lot of them are sometimes *far* too English for their own well-being—I mean, have you ever tried to talk with an English person about their feelings? It is IMPOSSIBLE—but they are not that bad."

Odette raised her eyebrows. "You do realize that at least five of them are rappelling down the side of the building right now?" She gestured at the shadows dangling just above them.

---

[77] "Sorry and thank you and I promise I won't do it again I like your dogs by the way thank you."

"How is that 'not bad'? I mean, do they not know how to use stairs?"

"It is literally not bad," said Edie, watching them with a critical eye. "Sethi and Sabia Gopal are doing particularly well. They are doing a lot better than Eloise Taylor, who is, I think, the one just sort of dangling in the middle. She really is most talented at dangling. Grand-Mère, is this conversation over? I must tell them a better route for their descents and I must tell them now. There is a particularly useful gargoyle that they should be aware of. You can use it as an anchor point."

"Edmée . . ."

"I might even ask Good Sister Paulette to let me help in her class when we get back to the school. My class on barricades went so well, I imagine they will be desperate to let me teach another. I imagine they might even let me put together my own curriculum. Remind me to talk to Good Sister June when we are back."

"You are not going back," Odette said as she turned and headed into the château. "Come with me." She did not wait to see if Edie followed her.

Edie followed her. There really was no other option. "Of course I am not going back; I am following you," she said in her Most Tactful Tone. "But after that, of course I *am* going back. I go to the School of the Good Sisters, and that is in England and not France. I know you are very, very old, Grand-Mère, but you do remember this, yes? My home is there in the North Tower with Hanna and Calla. I know you have not met them yet, but Calla is the one who talks a lot about ducks and has a surprising tendency for people to try to kidnap her, and

Hanna is basically more book than person, so they are not *perfect*, but they are my best friends and . . ."

Edie's voice trailed off, for she had just realized where they were going. Odette had led her to a very particular room within the château and it was one that Edie had never thought she would see the insides of again. After all, she had only seen it once by accident and circumstance.[78]

"The painting room," she said slowly. "Why are you taking me here?"

Odette began to unlock the door.

"I will go to bed," said Edie, taking a step back from her. "Are we finished talking? Good. You can go and be with your paintings and I can go and tell Calla and Hanna where my room is because they will not know and they really should know." She was very aware that she was talking too much, but she couldn't stop. "It has been so nice getting to know you again but really I should be going now and so I shall . . ."

"Come in," said Odette, as she pushed the door open.

And because Edie was who she was, she did.

---

78 Back when she prevented the thief, remember? I do, and I haven't even had my first biscuit of the day yet. Honestly, I am very on it this morning.

THE PAINTING ROOM

Imagine a room. Wall. Ceiling. A door. Maybe a few windows. A floor. The usual sorts of things.

Now imagine every inch of those walls packed in so tightly with paintings that you can't see any of the wall itself, and the floor packed so full of statues and furniture that you can barely walk through. There was a statue made out of polished white marble in one corner and enormous vases pushed up against each other in another, whilst one of the windows was blocked off with an enormous grandfather clock.

"Find a seat," said Odette. She walked carefully over to the nearest sofa and sat down, placing her hands neatly in her lap. She looked a little bit like she was about to have her photograph taken. "Quickly now, if you please."

But Edie could not move. "Do you know something? We should not have all of this stuff just lying about," she said. It didn't make any sense to her. "It is no wonder that people keep trying to burgle you, Grand-Mère, if this is what is here for them. We should sell it; have you thought of that? Have you spoken to my parents about this? They know of a thousand charities and causes that could make use of the funds, I think.

You see, if we sell off just one of these pictures, we could sponsor a thousand charities, and have you thought about what we could do with the statues . . . ?"

"Nothing is getting sold," said Odette.

"But why is it here? It does not do any good like this. You cannot even see half of it."

She had a point. Several statues were piled so close to each other that you could only see a leg of one and the arm of another, and one corner had a pile of paintings in their frames just laid on top of each other. It was all a little bit like somebody had started to decorate a cake and never stopped.

Odette took a deep breath. "I didn't bring you in here to talk about this."

"But please then accept my advice about it," said Edie, as she sat down opposite her. There wasn't much space to sit in, but somehow she managed it. "I have been reading the criminal press for years now, and I am particularly knowledgeable about art thefts in particular. Would you like to hear my theory about the theft at the Isabella Stewart Gardner Museum? It involves an invisibility cloak and a particularly talented contortionist."

"I sent you away to that school to forget this sort of thing," Odette said slowly. Her eyes were fixed on Edie, judging her. "And now you come back and I see you haven't changed one bit. What have they been teaching you?"

"They have taught me ABSOLUTELY everything," said Edie. "Everything that matters, at least. I have advanced medical training courtesy of Good Sister Robin, whose adoptive parents were doctors and so she is particularly knowledgeable about

LUNGS and VENTRICLES, and thanks to Good Sister Paulette I can now duel my enemies with an épée.[79] Also I can bake a perfect butterfly bun,[80] make a poison dart,[81] fly a light aircraft in stormy weather,[82] and if all of that does not persuade you, then last term I even learned how to lead a revolution and save my best friend from being kidnapped."

Odette took a deep breath.

She closed her eyes.

"I'm taking you out of the school," said Odette. "You're not going back."

----

79 A very slender and very pointy sword.
80 The key is to whip your mixture and get a lot of air into it before baking.
81 Carefully.
82 Have a very good map.

WHAT HAPPENED NEXT

Edie did not move.

She did not even breathe for a moment.

A long, long moment.

THE LENGTH OF A MOMENT

Silence can only last so long when you have a part of you that is trying very desperately to breathe. It was that part of Edie that made her take three enormous breaths, one after the other, in an attempt to fill her lungs. And once she did that, all of her feelings rushed up to her head and made her feel like she was about to faint.

"You look like you are about to faint," said Odette. "Put your head between your legs."

"I am not about to faint."

"It looks like you are."

"No," said Edie. "It might look like I am, but technically this is shock. All I have to do is remain calm, control my breathing, and also stay warm." She reached out to the nearest chair, grabbed one of the blankets from it, and wrapped it around her shoulders. Almost immediately, a comforting sensation of warmth began to flare inside her. "I learned about shock at school, by the way, and you want to take me away from it?" A part of her could not finish the sentence. A part of her did not want to.

"I sent you there to become a respectable young lady," said Odette. "But you aren't. Your report from last term was awful. I heard about all of it. You led a revolution? An uprising? I could not believe any of it. I had to see you for myself. I wanted to see if it was true, and now I see that it is. You have not learned anything. Your attitude is worse than it was when you left here. I do not even think your parents would recognize you."

A little knife of pain slid inside Edie's heart. "They would *always* recognize me," she said. "And I think they would *love* it there. It would be better than my papa's school. He told me about how horrible it was."

"That was a good school," Odette said instantly. "And I sent him there for a reason. Can you imagine growing up here with the memories of everything he had lost?" She gestured at the building around them. "I sent him there to keep him safe, and it worked. I sent *you* to your school to keep you safe. To make you become the young lady I know you can be. I have had my concerns for a while but your report and seeing the other pupils in person . . . they have only convinced me. I chose the wrong school. You are not going back to it."

"I will *not* stay with you," said Edie. She felt her voice start to shake and took a deep breath. One of the first things she had learned from her parents was how to control her emotions. The key was to not let them control you. At least, the key was to try to not let them control you. Sometimes it was easier said than done. "I will tell my parents."

"No, you won't," said Odette. She leaned forward, intent. "You cannot. You do not know whereabouts in the world they are.[83] They have not been in touch with you for weeks. You are

83 This was true and also, somehow, wrong. Edie did not need to know whereabouts in the world her parents were, and they did not need to know exactly where she was. Their love was too fierce and true to be stopped by little details like that.

my responsibility and I will look after you to the best of my ability. I am fighting for you, Edmée, even though you don't think I am. I am trying to protect you."

Edie glanced toward the door. They were only a couple of footsteps inside the room and yet it seemed as if it was miles away. "You are not making any sense. I won't talk about this with you. I can't."

She stood up, but her grandmother was ahead of her. Quicker than Edie had ever seen her move, Odette stood up too and moved so that she was blocking her escape. The two of them locked eyes. Odette said, "Sit down."

"That school has taught me *everything*," said Edie. She dodged around Odette and made for the door. "I am not stopping to listen to this. I will not."

"You are a twelve-year-old girl. You should not be living your life like this. You think it is fun; you give me these tips on how to stop burglars, you stop your friends from being kidnapped—whatever that means!—but you are wrong. You spend your days fighting when I know you should run. Run far, run fast, and never stop. Because when you stop to fight, when you stop to try to right the wrongs of the world, you lose."

Silence; endless, enormous silence.

The sort of silence that would have worked on anybody but Edie Berger, who paused with her hand on the doorjamb and a question in her heart. "Why would you say that?" she said. "Grand-Mère? What are you talking about?"

Odette did not reply. She was too busy staring at a small painting on the wall directly opposite her. It was an apparently unremarkable painting of two young girls, mounted in a damaged and cracked wooden frame, and I do not think that you and I would have even noticed it at all.

But Odette did. She could not take her eyes off it.

Edie looked at the painting and then at her grandmother. "Grand-Mère?"

Odette still did not reply, for she was lost in her memories. And it was only after hours, when the room grew cold and her mind started to come back to her, that she remembered where she was. "Edmée," she said slowly. Her whole body ached with a sudden grief and pain. "Are you still here? Have you gone as well?"

But there was no answer; the room was empty.

THE SECRET OF BIG HOUSES IS THAT THERE IS ALWAYS SOMEWHERE TO TAKE YOUR BROKEN HEART

When she left her grandmother in the painting room, Edie climbed to the top of the château and out onto the roof.

She inched her way along the battlements and past the gargoyles until she was certain that she was completely alone and safe.

And then she began to cry as though her heart was breaking.

Which, in a way, it was.

EARLY ONE MORNING

Edie did not come down from the roof for several long hours. She stayed there through dinner, and through bedtime, and all the way until she heard the clock two floors down begin to strike midnight through an open window. It was only then that she eased her aching muscles into action and crept back into the world.

The château was still and quiet around her. Moonlight shone in from the windows and cast long, silver shadows across the floor. The lights of Paris still glowed in the distance, a thousand different colors, all of them soft and shimmery and looking like flowers that only bloomed in the nighttime. For a moment, Edie just stood there and let herself take it all in. She had missed this more than she had understood. This view. This world. She had not thought that it did, but Paris still held a little bit of her heart in it.

But Paris was not the School of the Good Sisters.

The château did not have the North Tower in it. It did not have Calla or Hanna or the first-years or freshly made crumpets for breakfast. It did not have a forest perfect for building dens in, nor flat roofs that you could sit on and watch the stars from. It did not have emergency custard creams tucked in every spare cupboard that could be found and it definitely didn't have a light aircraft that sometimes, if Good Sister Paulette was in a good mood and the conditions just right, the pupils were allowed to fly down to the village and back.

As Edie stood there and realized all of this, she realized something else.

There was a man walking across the lawn.

And he was a man who should not have been there.

A BRIEF NOTE FROM YOUR NARRATOR

Once upon a time, dear reader, I went to house-sit for a fellow nun. House-sitting does not mean that one perches on top of the house like a large and rather ungainly owl; rather, it means that somebody comes and stays in your house and looks after it while you are away. I had been invited to house-sit by Sister Clodagh,[84] who was on her way to set up a convent in the Himalayas. She needed somebody to water her potted plants whilst she was there, and I was that somebody. I was meant to stay for only a few days but I ended up staying for several weeks.[85]

One of the features of Sister Clodagh's house was her electronic bed. This does not mean that it was a robot but rather that some parts of it lifted and others went down, depending on which button you pressed. It was very pleasant, for example, when you had breakfast in bed because you did not have

....

84 *Clodagh* is pronounced "clo-da," just as Victoria sponge is pronounced "per-fect."

85 Obviously this decision had nothing to do with the rather delightful bakery that had opened in the village and, obviously, I am lying.

to pile a lot of pillows behind your head to make sure that you were sat upright.

One of the other features of her house was a cat. His name was Arnold Falcone for reasons that I was desperate to understand and yet had never quite plucked up the courage to ask. He was big and delightfully solid in that way that only gentleman ginger cats can be. He also had a habit of sitting on the remote control for the bed. And one morning he sat on it whilst I was still asleep.

I woke up to the curious sensation of being folded up in a bed, my legs being forced into a rather peculiar right angle to the mattress itself, and with Arnold Falcone sitting happily on top of my head.

And the way I felt then was precisely how Calla felt when Edie woke her up.

IN WHICH EDIE HAS AN OPPORTUNITY TO TELL HER FRIENDS, BUT DOES NOT

"Where have you been?" Calla said as she pushed Edie away before doing a heartfelt yawn. "We looked for you at dinner, which was amazing, and then we thought you were still talking with your nan and then the nuns were pulling *Look, just don't ask us* faces and when we checked your room, it was empty, and now here you are waking us up in the middle of the night and that *always* means something's going on, so what is it?"

Edie took a deep breath. There was a little part of her that wanted to tell Calla everything that had happened, but there was a bigger part of her that did not want to. Telling Calla would mean telling Hanna and that would mean telling them both about the fact that she was leaving the school, and that was something that Edie was not even ready to admit to herself.

Not yet.

And maybe not ever.

"I was busy," said Edie. "But enough of me. I need your help!" She grabbed one of Calla's spare pillows and threw it over at Hanna, watching with some satisfaction as it landed squarely on top of her head. "Oh, my aim truly is perfect. Hanna! Awaken! We have problems to solve. There is a man who should not be here and I suspect that he is one of the people who keeps trying to steal from us and so we must go and investigate and SOLVE things and possibly also get some hot chocolate from the kitchens to fortify our souls."

Hanna glared at her out of the corner of one eye. "I'd managed to dream myself all the way to Belle's library and now you've ruined it."

"You cannot dream of magnificent libraries when a real-life mystery awaits!" said Edie. "Come with me! Both of you! Fame and glory and potential death awaits! There is an investigation to be made! A thief to be studied! Or, perhaps, we must make more of an observation of him until we see precisely what is going on with him, and the more both of you stay in bed, the more likely it is we miss him. Get up, get up, and come with me. Come *on*. There is an adventure to have and—and there is nobody I would like to have it with more than you two."

And even though her voice broke a little when she said this final part, she hid it so well that neither Calla nor Hanna noticed.

THREE SMALL GIRLS AT THREE IN THE MORNING

The art thief was in the process of breaking into the château. His name was Raphael Gagnon, and this is not the first time you have met him.

Raphael, or Victor, as he had been known then, was behind all of the burglary attempts on the château. One attempt had been foiled by a small girl of our mutual acquaintance, another by the firmly disapproving quacks of Henri the duck, and another by several dogs jumping onto his head and biting at his nose, but Raphael had kept coming back. Even though it had taken years, he had not given up.

And on this night, he felt like he might at last be successful. The stars were bright enough to ensure that he was not stepping on anything that would make a noise, and the night was quiet and still. He walked through the gardens and all the way up to the château's front door, and the only thing he heard was his own breath echoing loudly in his ears. No dogs, no ducks. He had come prepared with a bag of dog treats in one pocket and a handful of duck pellets in the other, but it looked like he wasn't going to need them.[86]

....

86 You may be surprised to hear that bread is not good for ducks. In fact,

Nevertheless he took his time as he disabled the alarm systems and carefully picked the locks on the door to the château, and he checked again when he was inside and heard a sound from upstairs.[87] His failed attempts had taught him to be cautious and so he was. He scanned the darkness. He tried to ignore the pain of the still-healing scratches on his forehead from his last encounter, and it was only when he was quite sure that he was alone and not about to be attacked by a horde of guard animals that he continued over to the painting room.

At this point, technically he should have been discovered. After all, the château was much fuller than it had been for weeks, and all of the nuns were aware that something was afoot. The only problem was that the doors and walls of a very old building are thicker than any of them had realized, and so only the shrieking of a very loud and quite overexcited first-year would have woken any of the nuns who were dreaming of profiteroles and macarons and those tiny little buns that are very pretty but do not fill you up until you have had at least thirteen of them.

And even those nuns who were awake and supposed to have been patrolling the grounds did not discover him, for they had been distracted by the curious delights of the château kitchens. I do not know if you have ever been very excited by a

----

a duck's favorite things include crustaceans, insects, nuts, berries, and things like that. They are quite the fine diners and do enjoy going out for dinner with their friends. The only problem is that ducks do not have pockets so they have to put everything on their bill.

87 Maisie Holloway was fake-sleepwalking to scare the other people on her floor, and because she had not figured out the necessity of keeping her eyes open, she had just fake-sleepwalked into the wall. Loudly.

kitchen in your life (it is a peculiarly adult sensation, I think) so let me explain. Good Sister Honey is one of the best cooks that I have ever met. Her kitchens at the school are one of my favorite places in the world and are even better when she is cooking. There have been many times when I have lined up with the girls so that we might have the honor of testing one of her new recipes. And so we must not blame the fact that the kitchen had proven so tempting to her that she had instantly begun to cook, and we must also not blame the fact that Good Sister Gwendolyn had nobly offered her services as tester.

It is at this point that you may think that, even in the absence of two gastronomically diverted nuns, Raphael should have been discovered by the girls themselves. They were on their first night of a trip to Paris, after all, and such an exciting thing was not the sort of thing to willingly sleep through. Several of the first-years had made a pact to not sleep for the entire week, a venture that had been unfortunately ruined by the warm coziness of their bedrooms and the fact that they had just eaten a supper substantial enough to feed the entirety of Paris twice over.[88]

But if any of them *had* woken up or paused in their epicurious adventures, then none of what happened would have happened.

Raphael would not have managed to unpick the door to the painting room in record time. He would not have walked

---

88 It is because of the magnitude of this magnificent meal that Maisie Holloway had swiftly recovered from her fake-sleepwalking exploits and was already back in her own bed and contentedly dreaming about fish fingers.

inside the room with a little smile on his face. He would not have thought that, after years of trying for the painting, now was the night that it might happen.

And he would not have made the mistake of turning on the light.

For it allowed somebody who was far too fond of dramatic timing to make her move.

As Raphael stood there, he saw a chair in the corner of the room turn around to face him. It contained a small girl with a remarkable quantity of hair, flanked on one side by a girl with three freckles in the precise outline of a mallard's tertial feather and on the other side by a girl carrying a copy of *The Whitby Witches*.

"Hello," said the girl in the chair. "I have been waiting for you."

CONFESSIONS OF AN ART THIEF

"My name is Edie Berger," said Edie, who was rather enjoying herself. There was something so intensely satisfying about when adults were lost for words. "I am the heir to the château and you are trying to steal one of my grandmother's possessions. But, more interestingly than that, this is not the first time you have tried, is it, Victor?"

Raphael stared at her. He was not used to people recognizing him, for he had spent his life deliberately making himself unrecognizable.[89] "Who are you calling Victor?"

Edie smiled right back at him. "You, because we have met before. You told me your name was Victor when *clearly* it is something else. However! I am not here to question your inability to think under pressure! I have many other questions for you and I would like you to answer them. Please, do not look worried. I do not mean to hand you over to the authorities. I just want to talk, as one professional to another."

Raphael stared at her a little bit more. He was rapidly starting

---

89 In proof of this fact, he had spent the last few days being mistaken for a tree by the local population of pigeons. It had left him in quite the flap.

to question why he'd ever taken this job on in the first place. Not only had it been actual years, but the small girl that he'd thought he'd hallucinated was not a hallucination, and she'd brought reinforcements.

Hanna tucked her book inside her dressing gown pocket before smiling at him in a sympathetic manner. "Please answer her questions," she said. "Calla and I got woken up for this and I really was having a very good dream."

"But I don't know what to say," Raphael said slowly. He scratched his head, trying to think about what was happening. "You keep talking to me like I am a thief. I have not stolen anything."

Edie leaned forward, fascinated. "I am not an amateur, my dear sir. One of the first things my parents taught me was to understand the legal system. It is only when we understand the rules that we have the right to break them. You have broken several laws in even being here without permission, I think. So, if I have to quote law to you, I will. What about Article 132–73?[90] Or 132–74?[91] And what about the municipal law passed in Châteauneuf-du-Pape in October of 1954?"[92]

"Er," said Calla, who rather thought they were getting off the point a little. "Don't you think you should be actually

---

90 Breaking in.

91 Climbing over enclosures.

92 This is the anti-UFO Municipal Law, which says that UFOs, namely Unidentified Flying Objects, are not allowed to park or fly above Châteauneuf-du-Pape. Since this law applies only to Châteauneuf-du-Pape and not to the center of Paris, it wasn't technically relevant, but I do not think that Raphael was able to ask questions at this point.

asking him why he keeps looking at that painting over there? The one that's a bit ripped and has got a broken frame."

Hanna stared at the painting and then at Raphael. "I don't want to be rude," she said thoughtfully, "but are you sure you're a very good art thief? Shouldn't you be stealing something that's a little bit more expensive-looking? I have read a lot of books about this sort of thing[93] and not once do they go for the painting that doesn't look like it's worth much."

It was a very relevant question to ask. That room was packed full of glorious and shining things. The painting with the rip and the broken frame didn't look like it should have even been there.[94]

"How can you say that?" said Raphael. He was unable to stop himself from replying even though he'd only understood about half of what the girl had just said to him. "There is nothing here to match it. *Les Roses Blanches* is the most valuable painting in the entire collection."

"So that is what you want," said Edie. She studied the painting carefully. It was not particularly remarkable. The frame about it had broken in one corner, and the painting itself was half the size of the one next to it. The only positive thing about it was that it would be very easy for somebody to take

....

93 I have asked Hanna for a reading list on this topic and she recommends the following: *From the Mixed-Up Files of Mrs. Basil E. Frankweiler* and *The Guggenheim Mystery*. They are apparently best read with some jammie dodgers close to hand.

94 Normally one would have such things fixed, but this damage told the story of the painting and the adventures it had lived. And in a while, you'll know precisely what I mean by that.

away with them. It would just look like a parcel being taken to the post office. "Who painted it? Why is it so special? Is it by Picasso or somebody else like that?"

Raphael shook his head. "I can't have a conversation about this. I have a job to do and you are delaying the inevitable. Would it be all right if I tied you up now? I have to get you out of the way somehow."

"No thank you," said Hanna politely. "I mean, it sounds like an excellent offer, but honestly I don't want to be tied up and even if I *was*, it wouldn't last long. I went to kidnapping training when I was three and hostage training when I was four, and there are very few knots that I can't make my way out of."

"You won't be able to undo mine."

"Please. You're going to begin with a double dragon and perhaps then you'll attach a clove hitch, and I can undo them with my eyes closed."

"I will not," said Raphael, rapidly changing his mind.

"You don't actually have to tie anybody up," said Calla. "You can just go away and not come back."

Edie coughed in a Pointed Fashion. "Not until I take his business card," she said. "And I'd also like to connect on social media. I feel we could have some mutually beneficial opportunities."

"Who *are* you people?" said Raphael.

"More to the point," said Odette Berger, from the doorway. "Who are *you*?"

IN WHICH ODETTE DOES NOT WAIT FOR AN ANSWER TO HER QUESTION

Edie had seen her grandmother angry and she had seen her sad and a thousand other emotions in between, but she had never seen Odette look as if she might shatter with rage. It was like looking into the heart of a thunderstorm; a black cloud had wrapped itself around Odette's shoulders and her eyes sparked with lightning.

And as Odette entered the room, Edie slid out of her chair so that she was next to Hanna and Calla. Almost instinctively they took a step or two back, pressing themselves against the wall so they were out of the way.

But Odette only had eyes for Raphael. She advanced on him ferociously, somehow twice the size she normally was, and when she stood in front of him, she stamped her silver cane on the floor and said, "You are a thief."

Raphael's mouth opened.

"I do not want to hear anything," said Odette.

Raphael's mouth closed. He gave Edie a *Please Help Me* look.

Edie gave him an *It's Best Just to Shut Up Right Now* look.

"You have come to steal a painting from me and you shall

not have it," said Odette. "I am quite aware that you will try again tomorrow, and the day after that and the day after that, but you will fail. I have fought for this painting; I have bled for it and I will die for it. You will *not* have it." And the moment that she finished speaking, she stamped her cane into the floorboards one final time.

And stepped back, smiling, as three small dogs and a duck hurtled into the room.

THE FIRST DENIAL

Henri the duck flew into Raphael's head and started beating him with his wings, whilst Baron Arturo[95] bit Raphael's left ankle, Countess Ginevra[96] took the right, and Sir Indigo[97] engaged in the remarkable feat of climbing all the way up Raphael's back and licking his ears. For a wild few seconds, the room was full of barks, quacks, and shrieks, until Raphael somehow managed to free himself and run for the door, leaving a trail of feathers and fur flying behind him.

"I'll go after him," Edie said quickly.

"You will not," said Odette. She was breathing heavily and her eyes were bright. "The animals will see him off the prem-

---

95 Baron Arturo had been key in foiling the last attempted burglary at the château with the novel and yet quite effective technique of jumping from a great height onto the top of the burglar's head.

96 Countess Ginevra is a most independent young hound who once, when she was young, had a nap on a tour bus and found herself in the middle of Poland when she woke up. She had returned home full of stories of her adventures and also, tucked underneath her collar, a recipe for the perfect dumplings.

97 Because Sir Indigo's favorite meal is marmalade on toast, I can only imagine that this was quite the sticky situation.

ises. It is not the first time they have done this and it will not be the last. They know what they are doing."

"But you can't just let him go. There's still some information that we can get from him."

Odette made a strange, shuddering sort of gasp at that. "Information?"

"Edie, I don't think that was the best thing to say," said Hanna as she began to pick feathers up off the floor. "Perhaps you need to be more delicate and introduce that sort of thing after we've cleaned up."

"Why are you even talking?" said Odette. It was not the most tactful thing she had ever said, but it was not a tactful sort of moment. "What on earth are you all even doing here in the first place?[98] What makes you think you can deal with any of this? You should all be in bed!"

"They came because I asked them to," said Edie. "They are my friends." She studied her grandmother, not quite understanding why she was looking at her like that. "If you do not realize that, Grand-Mère, then I do not know what to say."

"Well, I know precisely what to say," said Odette. "Have you told them about our earlier conversation?"

"I have not," said Edie, with a sudden, sharp, sinking feeling inside her heart. She glanced at Calla and Hanna, and the look of blank confusion on their faces made her turn back to her grandmother. "Please do not do this, they do not know—"

But it was too late.

....

[98] "It's sort of what we do," said Hanna in a very quiet and under-her-breath sort of manner.

THREE NO MORE

"Edmée is leaving your school," said Odette. "She has not learned anything of use there, and so I am withdrawing her. She will not be going back with you at the end of the week. She is staying here."

Calla's jaw dropped.

Hanna's eyes widened, and instinctively she turned to look at Edie. "What did she just say?"

"I am leaving our school," said Edie. A part of her had wondered if she might cry when she told the others, but she did not. There were no more tears left inside of her. It was the strangest and saddest of sensations. She had never felt anything like it in her life.

Calla said, "Is it true?"

"Yes," said Edie. "All of it is true. All of it."

And then there was nothing else left to say.

THE MORNING OF A BRAND-NEW DAY

When Edie opened her eyes, she took a long while to remember where she was. It was only when she heard Hanna's muffled snores and the soft vibration of Calla's phone, signifying another message had been received from her mum in the middle of one of her adventures, that she remembered that she was in the room next door to her bedroom in France, and last night had been real.

All of it had been real.

Leaving school. The art thief. The painting. Her grandmother's dramatic-yet-well-timed entrance. The sight of several small dogs and a duck attacking a quite unnerved man. The way that her grandmother had told Hanna and Calla about not going back to the school. The way that Edie herself had confirmed it.

Her thoughts felt like water. Everything inside her head was moving too quickly for it to make sense. She couldn't hold on to anything, and that scared her. She was so used to being able to figure out a problem and make everything better. This didn't feel like the sort of thing that *could* be made better.

She closed her eyes again, wondering if that would help.

All she had to do was see the order in it all and then the answer would make itself known. And so she let herself see it all over again, all of it. The art thief. The painting. Her grandmother. Calla and Hanna. The dogs. The duck. All of them floating inside of her head. The art thief. The painting. Her grandmother. And then, suddenly, the voice of her mother talking to her as if they were in the same room.

"Everything has a solution," said Marianne in that quiet, firm way of hers. *"You just have to be able to let yourself see it. And if there is anybody who can see it, it is you. You have all the skills to do so. You always have."*

And the moment that she finished speaking, Edie opened her eyes and smiled.

She knew exactly what to do.

KNOWING WHAT TO DO AND HOW TO DO IT

"Calla," said Edie loudly. "Hanna. Wake up."

"Why are you even in here?" Hanna said from underneath her pillow.

"I decided to sleep in here to make sure that you were all okay," said Edie.[99] "Also, if you are answering me, that tends to suggest that you are awake. You cannot fool me. I *know* you. How long have you been reading?"

"From 'some pig' to 'terrific,'" replied Hanna as she lovingly placed her bookmark into *Charlotte's Web* and put it down. "But the fact that you're awake first tells me that you're not over last night."

....

99 I must take a moment to tell you precisely what this means. Calla and Hanna had been put in a small room next door to Edie's bedroom, big enough for two camp beds and no more. Somewhere between them going to bed and waking up, Edie had dragged a small mattress through from her room and pushed it into the last remaining bit of space. She will tell you the same thing that she told Calla and Hanna: She had done this because she wanted to make sure that they were okay. But between you and me, I think she did it because she needed to be with two of the people that she loved most in the world.

"And the fact that *you* brought it up tells me that you are not over it, either," said Edie.

"Of course I'm not," said Hanna. "You're one of my best friends. You were the first person I met at the school and even if you are occasionally the *most* annoying, you are also occasionally Quite All Right. I am not going back to school without you, Edie Berger, even if I have to drag you back myself."

The two of them shared a look.

"I love you a little bit," said Edie. "Not as much as macarons, for I cannot love anything as much as macarons, but *definitely* more than doughnuts filled with jam."

Hanna grinned before throwing a pair of socks across the room, hitting Calla neatly on the head. "Wake up," she said. "We have plotting to do."

Calla opened one eye and glared at the two of them. "I have been paying attention," she said, tapping out a reply to her mum's text.[100] "I figured out something was up when I heard somebody else snoring in here and it wasn't you, Han. But look—I know we have to do something about everything that's happening, but I don't know what that something is. What can *we* actually do about any of it?"

"I have a plan," said Edie. "My grand-mère sent me to school to pick up the skills to be a nice young lady. And now she is taking me out of school because she thinks I do not have them. What we need to do is persuade her that I *do* have the

---

100 *HELLO MUM I AM IN PARIS I LOVE YOU PS: WHAT TIME DO DUCKS WAKE UP? THE QUACK OF DAWN.*

skills. It is just that she does not understand them. Because she is very old."

"Edie," said Calla.

"Stay on the point," said Hanna.

"We are going to save the painting that the thief keeps trying to steal. We are going to keep it safe using our Remarkable Talents. Remarkable Talents that will prove to my grand-mère that this school is good and I should stay in it."

"Can we use talents like poison darts? Good Sister Gwendolyn taught me one that sends people straight to sleep and it is AMAZING."

"I suspect Edie means things like our remarkable skills and cunning and knowledge," said Calla, calmly ignoring Hanna. "We need to find out who's in that painting and who painted it. If it's considered to be valuable and is that special to Mrs. Berger and the thief, there needs to be a reason why. People don't actually just steal things that they're not interested in. There's always a reason for it. We just need to find that reason."

"We can look at the Louvre later today," said Hanna. "It's our first trip. Maybe there's going to be more about the artist there. We could figure out who paints like them."

Edie nodded. "An excellent plan. Before we go, however, we could do some research in our library. We have a lot of books and one of them might have something on the painting . . ."

A small squeak escaped from Hanna. She turned bright red and then bright white, all in one curiously spectacular second, before getting out of her bed and taking a step toward Edie. "What did you say?"

IN WHICH THE GIRLS GO TO THE LIBRARY

Hanna took a step back. "Holy Shirley Hughes," she said, wiping a single and quite beautiful tear from her face. "Oh, Edie, oh, you never said it would be so beautiful."

For the library was beautiful; no other word could have done it justice.

The room ran nearly the entire length of the château. The wooden floor glowed from the regular polishing and dusting that the cleaners gave it, and the enormous bookshelves ran from floor to ceiling. There was a balcony at one end, reached by a delicate spiral staircase, where yet more shelves were full to the brim with books. Some of them were new but the majority were old, with faded spines and sun-bleached covers. Every now and then, there was a shelf that had a thin grille of metal in front of it as a barrier.

"Those are the absolutely rarest of the books," said Edie. "I think they belonged to my noble relative Luc Berger and, after he died, my grand-mère had them all put away up here and has never looked at them since. Honestly, why is everything about my life so *incredibly* gothic and fabulous?"

"I think you are getting off the point," said Calla.

"Indeed I am!" said Edie, who had never met a conversational side path that she did not love intensely. "Some of the books here are hundreds of years old. I never was allowed to look through them. I was never even allowed *in* without permission. There has to be something here about the painting, but I do not know where to begin."

"Luckily enough, I do," said Hanna. She had been standing by the nearest shelf dreamily studying the titles. "Look at the way that the spine's cracked on this book and how the pages are all crumpled in it. We want the books that are about art, but we also want the books that have been *read*. If there is anything about that painting here, it will be in a book that's been read. You want to know about the things that you have. But it's not here. Even though they've been read, this isn't the right shelf. Hang on."

Hanna began to move down the shelves, studying them intently. She shook her head at one row of books and then pulled a face at another. "These are books about animals and travels. And these are too old. Wait, these ones are too small. We need art books and they don't often look like this. They're really big. Hang on and let me look up here." She climbed up the spiral staircase and then let out a small whoop of victory. "Got it. This shelf. It's nothing *but* art books."

Edie and Calla raced up the stairs after her. They found Hanna standing in front of the biggest bookshelf of all. It ran from the floor to the ceiling, as all of the others did, but the shelves were the length of at least six first-years laid end to end. As she stood there, Edie realized that even Calla—the tallest of the three of them—would have to sit on somebody's shoulders to reach the top shelf.

Which was just as full, if not fuller, than all of the others.

"Isn't it *beautiful*?" Hanna said in awe. "If I'm not on the bus at the end of this week, I'm going to be here making myself a fort made entirely out of books and you are *not* allowed to come and find me except to bring me a bowl of bigos."[101]

Calla shook her head. She looked concerned. "I haven't had my breakfast yet. We're going to need help."

"And I know exactly where to find it," said Edie. "Come with me."

---

101 This is the Polish word for a special sort of stew. All stews are special, but bigos is particularly so.

IN WHICH THE FIRST-YEARS' ALARM CLOCK GOES OFF

"Good morning, everybody! It is time to wake up, cry havoc, and let slip the dogs of war![102] Yes, I *know* there are no dogs, Sethi, but it helps to think *metaphorically* about this sort of thing and not just yawn and look at me with a vacant expression. That is better! Well done, you! Everybody else! It is time for you to also pay attention! Also, if somebody could please poke Maisie Holloway in the side and ensure that she is properly awake rather than *pretending* to be and sneakily having an extra snooze, I would appreciate it!

"Perfect. Thank you. Okay. Let us begin!

"Hello!

"My name is Edie Berger, and you are all currently in my house in Paris! And I *know* that you haven't had breakfast yet, and that you should have at least another two hours in bed, but there is a mystery afoot. And we need your help solving it. By 'we,' I mean Hanna and Calla and myself, the most

....

102   This is a quote from a play called *Julius Caesar*. It was written by William Shakespeare, who was a very good writer. I suspect he would have made an excellent fruitcake as well.

remarkable three members of the North Tower bedroom. And by 'you,' I mean all of you first-years, even the ones I have not yet learned to identify by name because you just do not stand still long enough for me to do so. You are Quite Numerous!

"We need you to come on a QUEST with us! We need to find something out in the library and there isn't enough time, but we will do it if you all come and help us! I *know* it sounds a little bit like we might be asking you to do extra work on what is *technically* a holiday but it is all for a good reason, and that good reason is—it is—"

And here Edie's voice faltered for the first time since she had begun.

I think it was, perhaps, for the first time ever.

WHEN YOUR BEST FRIEND SAYS IT FOR YOU

But then Calla stepped forward.

"Edie is being taken out of the school," she said quietly. "Her grandmother is convinced that the school isn't good for her and so, when we go back home at the end of this week, Edie won't be with us. She'll be staying here."

A low moan of anguish went around the room: Several of the first-years began to cry, one of them swooned from the shock of it all, while another small and quite passionate individual said, "I'LL STAY INSTEAD OF HER; I'LL SACRIFICE MYSELF."[103]

"It's up to all of us to save Edie," said Calla, calmly ignoring everybody. "Her grandmother thinks the school doesn't teach useful things, so we're going to prove that it does. We're going to figure out why somebody keeps trying to steal one of the paintings downstairs and we're going to stop him because we're very good at that sort of thing. And when we do that, Mrs. Berger will see how great the school is and why Edie

---

103   This was Emily Greenwood, who, you may be interested to know, has the peculiar talent of being able to stand on one leg and recite the alphabet backward. Please do not ask me how she discovered this.

should stay with us. We need your help. Now, pretty much. Will you come with us?"

For a long and vivid moment, nobody moved.

Edie took a deep breath. She placed her hand on Calla's arm. She looked toward the door. A part of her wanted to walk right through it.

And then Lucy Millais stood up and stopped her right where she was. "I'll help you," she said. Her voice rang proudly around the bedroom, packed with first-years. "I helped you out last term, didn't I? I was *pivotal* in sorting things out. So, I'm not going to back out now. This is what we do in this school. We help people. And if you need us, Edie, I'm right there."

"Me too," said Eloise Taylor. She bounced to her feet to stand next to Lucy. The two of them gave each other a friendly grin. "Edie, we're not leaving you here. You're one of us. If your granny needs help in realizing that, then count me in."

The floodgates opened then. One by one the first-years stood up, all of them pledging themselves to the cause. Sethi and Sabia Gopal made their pledges at the same time;[104] Thea de Grazie stood up without realizing that Ellen Beaufort had tied her laces together;[105] and several of the tiniest and most indistinguishable first-years grabbed Edie around the legs and refused to let go.

And once they had been disentangled,[106] Calla pointed at the door. "All right then," she said. "Let's get started."

....

104 Understandably so, because they were identical twins.
105 And so she fell over, rather swiftly, but not without taking Ellen along with her for the ride.
106 I do not know if you have ever had to disentangle a cat from a ball of wool, but disentangling the first-years from Edie was a rather similar process.

A LATE BREAKFAST WITH GOOD SISTER JUNE

It was not often that Good Sister June mislaid a substantial number of pupils.

She had, of course, mislaid the odd individual child but tended to find them again without much difficulty.[107] When Edie had run away, back when she had first joined the school and hated every inch of it, Good Sister June had found her hiding in the rooms between the walls of the school. And at the start of this term, when three particularly nervy first-years managed to get themselves lost between their classroom and their bedroom,[108] she had found them in the school kitchens drinking freshly made hot chocolate with marshmallows on top. She had not, however, expected to lose thirty-seven girls (three of whom were members of the same bedroom) on their first morning in Paris. And she had definitely not expected to lose thirty-seven girls when breakfast was being served.

She went off to investigate what had happened to them,

---

107 It turns out that the best way to find a missing first-year is to simply open a fresh packet of biscuits. It is even more productive if you have one of those biscuits for yourself.

108 A surprisingly simple journey, you might think, but first-years are first-years.

armed with an emergency brioche in one hand and a mug of coffee in another. Her brioche lasted as long as the hallway, where she ran into Good Sister Gwendolyn's impromptu survival skills class.[109]

Or, to be more precise, when she ran into an armchair that said, "Ow."

"Is that you, Lily Maguire?" said Good Sister June.

The armchair looked disappointed. "It is. How did you know?"

"I am your *headmistress*," said Good Sister June splendidly, taking another bite of her brioche. "Also, your foot is showing. I have seen many curious things in my life but I have never seen an armchair with slippers."

"Aha," said the armchair. "Noted. Good Sister Gwendolyn did tell us to be careful about that."

Good Sister June left Lily contorting on the ground floor and headed on up the stairs. She had learned a long time ago that mischief and mayhem tended to happen as far away from the adults as possible. Thirty girls[110] missing from a meal (a distinctly rare occurrence in the history of the School of the Good Sisters) meant that something along those lines was clearly happening and so Good Sister June climbed the stairs toward the top of the château to look for them.

Where a small girl stood, waiting for her.

"Hello, Good Sister June," said Edie Berger. "I've been expecting you."

---

109 And, in the process, locating seven of her missing pupils.
110 You will note that she had already found seven.

AN UNEXPECTED REACTION

Edie led Good Sister June into the library, explaining everything as she did so. She was happy to see that the nun seemed to be taking it all surprisingly well. Between you and me, this is because Good Sister June was rather impressed at how several first-years kept scuttling in and out of the room with fresh pastries and hot drinks for the other girls, and was debating the ethics of adding "first-years doing useful stuff like this" to the school curriculum on a permanent basis.

"You are very quiet," said Edie severely. "I *had* thought that telling you that I was leaving would be much more dramatic. I expected some tears, at least."

"I am thinking," said Good Sister June, rapidly deciding to focus upon the matter at hand. She walked over to the part of the library where Hanna was sitting, surrounded by books and first-years. "Hanna, hello. I presume you have a guidebook somewhere about your person?"

"I don't know what that means," said Hanna.

"It is a fancy way to say 'close to hand,' which is also a fancy way of saying 'near to you,'" said Good Sister June. "Nuns are very fond of fancy words, I know, but usually the rest of the sentence can give you a clue as to what they mean."

"Oh," said Hanna. She studied the books that were closest to her before gesturing at one pile in particular. "There are some guidebooks here that mention the art museums. If that's what you mean? I thought we could start by trying to see if any of the other paintings in them looked similar to the one downstairs. I know we're going to the Louvre later and can kind of look in person, but the books . . ."

"Do any of them mention the Marché au Puces de Saint-Ouen?" said Good Sister June.

"Yes," said Hanna. She reached out and grabbed a slender volume from the top of the pile and waved it in the air. "This one. It says that it's the world's largest market of secondhand stuff and antiques. Each street has a specialty, so, for example, you could go down one that sells only pictures of brioche or down another one that only sells cake stands. I mean, I'm not sure that there's *specifically* an alley that's just for cake stands or pictures of brioche, so it's better if you consider it as an idea of what to expect *rather* than as an actual example. Anyway, it's the place to go if you want to buy nice old things and find out about them because there are a lot of people there who know precisely about this sort of thing and OH—!" Hanna gasped and fell silent.

"Indeed," said Good Sister June.

"What is going on?" said Edie. "I do not understand. Why do you all look like you have stomach problems? And why on earth are you smiling like that, Hanna?"

"She is smiling because she has figured out what we are going to do today," said Good Sister June, who had rapidly decided to focus on that and not the comment about her digestive system. "Good Sister Christine is going to take a third of you to the Louvre this morning. Good Sister Gwendolyn is going to spend the morning with her students at the château so that she can take full advantage of the grounds for her covert-skills class. And *I* am going to take the rest of you to a market where people might know a lot about antiques. In particular, they might know a lot about paintings that need saving in order to save a pupil at my school from being taken away from us. Does that sound like a plan?"

A passing first-year burst into rapturous applause.

"I'll take that as a yes," said Good Sister June.

ARRIVING AT THE MARCHÉ AU PUCES DE SAINT-OUEN

The first thing that you should know about the flea market at Saint-Ouen is that it is not just one flea market. It is several markets that are stretched over miles of twisting and inter-locking streets in the very heart of Paris. Some of the market is outside in the open air and some of it is inside tiny shops or in the middle of vast and airy buildings; some of it is displayed against the painted garage doors in the street and some of it is set out on a table that somebody has borrowed from their parents' attic. One road sells nothing but old oil paintings, framed in gold and bigger than anything that Edie had ever seen in the château, whilst another sells nothing but tables of all shapes and sizes piled so haphazardly up against the walls, you can't help but wonder how they managed to stay there and not fall down. A small side street sells antique toys, whilst a street in the other direction sells china cups and saucers, and the street that joins the two sells nothing but richly colored carpets. And in the middle of all of this are a substantial number of small and delicious-smelling restaurants with chalkboards propped up outside of their door and the menu for the day already writ-ten on it.

It is one of my favorite places in the entire world and I love it greatly.

Good Sister Paulette parked the bus next to a particularly delightful-looking patisserie. More innocent tourists might have seen this as a coincidence, but arranging one's holiday around delightful-looking patisseries is a key part of the curriculum at the School of the Good Sisters.[111] As Good Sister Paulette opened the bus doors and Good Sister Robin took the opportunity to start singing a song,[112] Good Sister June stood up to speak to the girls. "We have arranged for you to spend the morning here at the market, and elevenses at this patisserie, La Belle Gateau.[113] It is the best patisserie in the area, because we are professionals at this sort of thing, and it also does a rather remarkable chocolate éclair. I hope that this is incentive enough to not get lost and be back on time. If you require further incentive, not being back will mean that you miss elevenses and also lunch and possibly also dinner."

A low cry of horror escaped the first-years, who had definitely paid attention to that. One particularly nervous tiny child inhaled dramatically before falling off her seat, whilst another, sitting across the aisle from Edie, said, "I've *never*

---

111 Along with Working Out the Correct Proportion of Icing to Cake (lots); The Importance of Impromptu Afternoon Snoozing (very); and The Benefits of a Well-Timed Biscuit (immeasurable).

112 She really does get very excited.

113 *La Belle Gateau* means "the beautiful cake." I know it is a quite on-the-nose sort of name, but really I think it is very good.

missed a lunch," and wiped a tear from her eye at the mere thought of such horrors.

"Off you go then, girls," said Good Sister June.

And so they did.

A QUITE CONFUSING ENCOUNTER

I am conscious that the last chapter made it all sound very straightforward, so here is the part where I tell you the truth. Books that feature mysteries to be solved do tend to have clues popping up all over the place. Real life is nothing like that and so, perhaps inevitably, the girls were struggling in solving theirs.

"It's like we're looking for the Scarlet Pimpernel,"[114] said Hanna, after one particularly fruitless encounter. "If we were the Secret Seven or the Famous Five, we would have clues practically everywhere we looked."

"Also that last man we spoke to didn't understand a word I said," replied Calla—who had, to be fair, spoken to him in a mixture of French, English, and slightly panicked mime.

Edie grinned. "That is because your French is appalling. It is like you have socks in your mouth or something. You must have more flair when you say everything. Perform the words

---

114 This is a very exciting book written in 1905 about a man who was a little bit like Batman. I am not sure what that really means, but Good Sister Gwendolyn has told me it is the best way to describe it to you all, and so I have.

like they've never been spoken before." She paused and looked thoughtful. "Really, you should just be more French. Can you work on that a little bit, please?"

"But I'm English and this is the first time I've been out of the country," said Calla. "Why am I even doing the conversations when you are actually, literally real-life French?"

"Because I am looking for *clues*," said Edie, who had thought this was obvious. She nibbled the edge of her *crêpe au chocolat*[115] delicately. "It is not just in what people tell us, it is about how they say it. And if they say something to you that sounds believable while making a face that says quite the opposite, then I shall see it thanks to my astute skills in subterfuge."

"Excuse me," said the stall owner that they'd been having this conversation by the side of all along. "Are you all going to buy something, or . . . ?"

"I am on *holiday*," said Hanna brightly. "Of course we are going to buy things. But first, we want to ask you for some help. We're looking for information about a painting."

The man shrugged. "Well, you're in the right place. We do nothing *but* paintings in this part of the market. Does this one of yours have a name? Or do you know who painted it?"

"We don't know who painted it," said Calla. She glanced at Edie, wondering if she wanted to say something, but Edie shook her head and waved her on. She was too busy thinking. "I can describe it to you, though. There's two women in it, and they're looking straight at you. It's kind of small and—"

....

115 This is a very thin pancake with a lot of chocolate spread on it, so basically the most perfect snack ever invented. Except for jammie dodgers.

"*Les Roses Blanches*," he said, cutting in before she could finish her description of the painting. "You're talking about *Les Roses Blanches*. Every artist in the city knows about that painting. It's by an artist named Kurt Mercier and it went missing after the Second World War, along with much of the rest of his collection. Most of his paintings have been found now, but that one hasn't. It's practically mythical. People have spent their whole life looking for it."

And all of a sudden everything started to make sense to Edie Berger. "Thank you," she said. "You have been *most* helpful."

MEANWHILE, AT THE LOUVRE

Things were going less well.

They had *begun* quite well. Lucy Millais had gathered their branch of the "Save Edie from Being Thrown Out of School" club outside of the Louvre and delivered a very inspiring speech. Part of this speech had involved a five-minute lesson on how to knead dough and, although the relationship to the task at hand was rather unclear, the girls had happily practiced what they had learned before going inside the museum itself.[116] In there, they had split up into smaller groups with the aim of finding out more about *Les Roses Blanches*. Some of the girls joined Good Sister Christine in a conversation with one of the art curators in order to find out more information, while several others had decided to buy themselves a second breakfast in the hope that clues lay within their cafeteria of choice.

This had left Lucy Millais, Maisie Holloway, and several

---

116 I will leave you to imagine what this looked like, considering that the girls were standing in the middle of the street and had nothing in the way of actual real-life ingredients near them. Let me just say, it made several of the nearest tour groups decide to go up the Eiffel Tower instead.

tiny first-years walking through the museum, and when they had gotten to the *Mona Lisa* room, they had made their way through to the front and studied the painting with interest. It did not look anything like *Les Roses Blanches* and so they had crossed Leonardo da Vinci off their list, before having a feverish debate over what Mona Lisa's favorite biscuit might be.

And all along, Maisie and Lucy had tried to ignore the fact that they were being followed by a duck.

YOU CAN'T IGNORE A DUCK FOREVER

Things came to a head when they entered one of the quieter wings of the museum. Lucy pulled Maisie to the side of the room, just next to a beautiful carving made entirely out of marble, and said, "THERE IS A DUCK FOLLOWING US AND I THINK IT IS NOW TIME FOR THE SITUATION TO COME TO A HEAD."

(Forgive me for all the capital letters but it was a capital-letters sort of moment.)

"I don't know what 'come to a head' means," Maisie said calmly, for she was somebody who was very good at staying calm during Capital Letters moments. It was a skill that she had honed over many years of being the elder sibling of three younger brothers who had a marvelous talent for getting into complicated problems. "Let's stand here and pretend we're interested in this painting of a very old white man and try to figure things out. First of all, I think we can begin with the fact that there is a duck in the art museum and nobody seems to be bothered."

"That's a good point," said Lucy. "Nobody is bothered by the fact that there's a duck here. And they are definitely not even bothered by the fact that it's *queuing*."

This was a very accurate description of the situation. The duck had lined up behind a queue for one of the more popular exhibits and was quietly waiting its turn to see the painting without anybody standing in front of it. Maisie and Lucy watched it stand in front of the painting as though it was looking right at it, and when it was done, it looked left and then right before walking over to their side of the room. For a moment it was just the three of them, before a great tour group came through. Maisie and Lucy stepped back to let them pass, losing sight of the duck as they did, before suddenly the room was empty again and all that was left on the floor was a piece of paper and a single, solitary duck feather.

"We should pick it up," said Lucy, for she was the sort of person who would always pick up potentially mysterious notes on the floor. "It might be something important."

And it was.

WHAT THE NOTE SAID

Ask Odette Berger about Agathe Mercier.

MEANWHILE, BACK AT THE MARKET

"We need to go over the clues one more time," Hanna said thoughtfully. "That's what they'd do in *Murder Most Unladylike* and it works for them, so it might work for us. What do we have?" She looked thoughtful. "Kurt Mercier. A priceless painting. And the fact that nobody knows where it is, but we know that it's in your front room. Isn't that a bit weird?"

"First of all, they are adults, so *clearly* that is a factor," replied Edie. "Secondly, how could anybody know about it? My grand-mère has never let anybody be in the same room as it before. Not even me. She used to go in there and lock the door behind her. I only got in because I made a copy of the key."

"I think we need to know more," said Calla.

"Making a copy is *so* straightforward! First, you need something like soap to press the key into so that it molds it and then—"

Calla poked Edie. "That is *not* what I meant."

"What we need to do is think about the practicalities," said Hanna, calmly ignoring all of this. "You have to think about how the moment that somebody tries to steal the painting, they're stuck with it. You can't quietly sell a painting that everybody knows about and that *everybody* will know is stolen. I'll bet that the thief is working for somebody who wants it all for themselves."

"Exactly like my grand-mère," said Edie.

Hanna nodded. "Like—weirdly like her."

The two of them stared at each other.

And then Calla said something quite unexpected. "Out of interest, do you two see that duck?"

THE MAGNIFICENT TIMING OF A PARISIAN DUCK

Calla took a step forward. Her eyes were bright and she looked deeply intrigued. "It's the duck from the château. I wonder what it's doing here?"

"But how on earth do you know that?" said Edie. She gave Calla a look of genuine interest. "You have seen my grand-mère's duck but once, Calla, my unique little *pomme de terre*. Are you really telling me that you can recognize it again? It is a remarkable skill of yours if you can. I must make more use of it. Perhaps we could explore some crime scenes together."

Calla nodded. "One of the first games I ever remember playing with my mum was Duck Snap. She drew pictures of ducks, and I had to match them up. We did it a lot. I got so good that I could practically pair ducks with my eyes closed. I am telling you, that's the duck from the château. And I'll tell you something else. It's a Qvada duck. Just look at the color of its speculum.[117] When it attacked the thief last night, that's

....

[117] This is the fancy word for the colorful bit on the bottom of the duck's wing. You will see it best when the duck is flying and the wing is outstretched. Other ways of identifying a duck include looking at their bills, the shape of their heads, and their eating habits. This last one also works well on humans, I think.

157

when I first saw it. I'll never forget it. It's completely unique, actually. No other duck in the world looks like that. My mum would be absolutely unconscious with excitement over it."

"You're like a superhero," said Hanna, awestruck. "But one with a really odd and very specific skillset."

Edie did not say anything, for she was too busy thinking. She had the sneaking suspicion that her grand-mère would not approve of the duck wandering around the market by itself, and even if it did have her permission, a duck strolling around a flea market was most unusual behavior. She also had the sneaking suspicion that the duck was worthy of paying attention to because of this.

Suddenly she came to a decision, and the swift and sudden sense of satisfaction inside of her heart told her that she had made the right call. She pulled Hanna and Calla over to the side of the path and, out of the corner of her eye, she registered how the duck watched them do this. It did not look at them directly, nor did it even turn its head, but she *knew* it was watching them. "We are going to go over to it and help it," she said. "It might be lost and need our help. So! We shall help it."

"We don't have time," said Hanna. She pulled a little face at the others. "I'm sorry, but we don't. We are meant to be investigating the painting and there's not long before we need to be back at the patisserie."

Calla crouched down so she was eye level with the duck. She looked intrigued. "You know, it actually looks like it's watching us. Maybe it recognizes us from the château. Ducks are really smart creatures. They can figure out the difference between things like that." And then all of a sudden, she stopped speaking and instead made a curious sound that was somewhere between a squeak of disbelief and a gasp of excitement.

The duck was coming toward them.

SERIOUSLY, YOU REALLY CAN'T IGNORE A DUCK FOREVER

It was then that something quite unexpected happened. Calla reached out her hand toward the duck, which was, indeed, walking in their direction. She retracted her hand quite quickly when a bus pulled over in front of her and began to unload a substantial number of tourists. Edie and Hanna grabbed her and the three of them stood back so that they were out of the way. The only problem was that the tourists did not move far. A substantial number of them had to get shopping bags out of the luggage compartment of the bus, whilst several others managed to cross the road and then looked quite lost, whilst another group simply sat down at the nearest café and began to order.

"Oh, this will not do," Edie said suddenly. She took a deep breath and stepped firmly into the crowds of people in front of them. Within minutes, Calla and Hanna heard her ordering people forward and making them move out of the way. She sent one group down a street packed full of fabric stalls and rolls of material gleaming in the sun, and another group headed off toward a street where every stall sold brightly polished pots and pans. I do not think any of the tourists quite knew what had happened to them, but I suspect it was a good thing that *something* had happened, otherwise they might still be there even now.

When Edie came back over, the driver gave her a grateful thumbs-up before getting back into his bus and moving it. She gave him a thumbs-up in return and then, suddenly, the street was empty and it was as if the last ten minutes had never happened.

The only thing that was left was a folded-up piece of paper and a solitary duck feather.

THE SECOND NOTE

Ask Odette Berger about Agathe Mercier.

CHOUX HEARTS AND REALIZATIONS

It will not surprise you to know that after all of this, Edie, Calla, and Hanna missed their elevenses at the patisserie. There was a very tense moment when it looked like they might miss their lunch as well, because they were very busy staring at each other and saying things like "Was that note meant for us?" and "Who's Agathe Mercier?" and "Is she anything to do with Kurt Mercier?" but then Calla said, "Shouldn't we be actually heading back to the patisserie by now?" and Hanna said, "Oh my god, I've eaten my sock biscuit!" and the three of them realized that they should return before they expired of hunger.

They were greeted at the patisserie by Good Sister June, who led them over to some empty chairs in the corner of the room. "I saved you some food," she said. "You really are most remarkably late. I had to hold Good Sister Gwendolyn back from eating your cake."

"Thank you," said Edie. She pushed Calla and Hanna forward so that they could help themselves first, and she had to make only the smallest of coughs when Calla almost helped herself to a macaron that she wanted. Once Calla selected the correct cake, and Hanna was sitting down and getting updates from the first-years who had been exploring the rest of the market, Edie picked up her macaron and turned to Good Sister June. "We have had a strange morning," she said slowly, deciding to not mention the note for now. It still seemed too much of a coincidence that it could be connected to the painting or to whoever Kurt Mercier was. "Everybody knows about the painting but they all think that it disappeared in the war. It was painted by a man named Kurt Mercier."

"Do you know who that is?" said Good Sister June.

Edie shook her head. "I have never heard of him."

"Well, we can try to find out more in the Musée d'Orsay this afternoon. There has to be somebody who knows more about the painting or this Kurt. Maybe he's mentioned somewhere."

"But what if he isn't?" Edie said very slowly. "One must always admit the possibility of defeat, my dear Good Sister, and I think I have had defeat on my mind ever since you came over and told me that my grand-mère had offered us the château to stay in. She always wins. It is like she is two or three steps ahead of me, all along, and I can never catch up."

Good Sister June studied her small and remarkable pupil for a long moment. "I don't know what to tell you." It was not something she would have admitted to many other pupils in her school, but Edie was the sort of pupil who demanded truth. Even when it was not the sort of truth that one should ever say.

"I know," said Edie. She reached out and helped herself to another macaron, pushing the plate over to Good Sister June.

"That is what makes you a good adult. All of the others would be telling me positive things like 'You will solve this mystery' and 'It's always darkest before dawn,' but you do not, and I am grateful for it." She heaved a sigh and decided to change the subject. It was all far too depressing. "Look, Good Sister June, if it is all right with you then I will go down to the Rue de la Vérité tonight and take Calla and Hanna with me. I would like to show them my maman's plant shop and maybe somebody on the street will know something that can help us out in our quest."

Good Sister June smiled. "You have my permission," she said. "And do remember: This is only the first day, Edie. No battle is ever won in the first round. You know that better than most."

"I do know that," said Edie, "but one thing I do not know is why Hanna is making that most remarkable expression at us."

Good Sister June twisted round to see what was happening. She had thought that Hanna was contentedly eating a choux heart full of sweet vanilla custard, but that was very far from the truth. Hanna had definitely begun to eat her choux heart, but she had pushed it aside half finished, and that— along with the stunned expression on her face—told Good Sister June that something very unusual had happened. She glanced across to where Calla was busily talking away on her phone, her chocolate éclair forgotten on her plate, and the same expression on her face. The moment that she finished her call, Calla placed her phone back into her pocket and went over to talk to Hanna. The two of them shared a quick conversation before getting up and coming over to join Edie and Good Sister June. The éclair and the choux heart were left abandoned behind them.

"Something has happened," said Edie calmly. "Tell us what it is."

IN WHICH THINGS START TO COME TOGETHER

It was Calla who began. "So, I just got off the phone with Lucy and Maisie. I thought I'd ring them to get a quick update."

"And I just talked to the first-years," said Hanna, rapidly finishing off her chocolate éclair. "They were all looking through the market and asking people, same as us, and I wanted to know how they'd got on." She reached out to grab a passing jam tart. "Raspberry!"

Calla helped herself to a mysterious-looking choux pastry. She took a quick bite and then said with some delight, "Chocolate! Anyway, Lucy and Maisie got Good Sister Christine on the call as well. They put me on speaker. Everyone could hear me and I could hear all of them."

"Turns out that the first-years got the same story in the market that we did. Exactly the same. They spoke to literally hundreds of people between them, and they were getting nowhere."

"Everybody said the same thing. Kurt Mercier. Missing painting. Practically priceless in every way. Nobody knows where it is. And that was *it*."

"But then one of the first-years said something that I found unexpectedly interesting—"

"And just before I was going to hang up, Lucy and Maisie said something weird."

"The first-years found a note—"

"And so did Lucy and Maisie—"

"And they saw the duck before they found the note—just like we did."

"And they thought it was just a coincidence, but—"

"It can't be a coincidence."

"Because you'll never guess what it said?"

Edie leaned forward, her mind racing. "I think I might," she said, unfolding the piece of paper and placing it in the table in front of them. *Ask Odette Berger about Agathe Mercier.* Six simple words. And here they were, about to change everything.

THE MARVELOUS MIND OF MADEMOISELLE BERGER

Good Sister June raised her eyebrows. "Another Mercier. Is that a coincidence?"[118]

"No," said Edie, after a long, thoughtful pause. "It is fate." It was all starting to make sense. Paris was her city, her home, and she understood the things that happened in it as well as she understood her own heart. One note on the streets of Paris might have been something to ignore, but the same note appearing in three different locations? And mentioning somebody who shared the same surname as the person who'd painted *Les Roses Blanches*? That was definitely something to pay attention to.

"Nothing happens by chance," said the voice of Edie's mother suddenly inside her head. They had been walking down the street as part of a great crowd of people protesting climate

....

118 There were a lot of things that Good Sister June could have done at this point. She was, after all, the Responsible Adult, and Responsible Adults would have done things like checking the girls' temperatures and reminding them that ducks can't write before asking them to not talk and eat at the same time. But those sorts of adults were dull and boring and Good Sister June was a headmistress who was not.

change, flags and placards being carried beside them. Edie had been only a handful of years old but she had marched with the rest of them, full of glory and excitement at being part of it. "People might think that a protest like this happens by chance, but it does not. It happens because of people who listen to what the world tells them. All you have to do is be able to listen."

Edie nodded. "We must speak with my grand-mère," she said.

THE SEVEN WORDS THAT CHANGED EVERYTHING

Odette Berger had not expected to be disturbed for several hours. She had watched the girls set off in their bus, locked the door after them, and then, tired in a way she could not quite understand, she had returned to the painting room and dozed, surrounded only by the dogs. Once when she opened her eyes, the duck was there too, watching her, but the next time she opened her eyes he had disappeared and she was left thinking that she had dreamt him being there in the first place.

When the door of the château opened and she heard the sound of her granddaughter and her friends in the hall, Odette thought she was dreaming that, too. It was only when there was a gentle knock on the door that she realized it was actually happening. She said, "Yes—" and "Don't come in" and "I'm coming," all of this somehow at the same time and in the same breath, before she eased herself awake and made herself stand up and walk out of the painting room.

Her muscles ached. Her heart ached too. Even standing was an effort, and when Edie offered her an arm for support, Odette had to take it to stop herself from falling. "What are you doing here?" she said. "I thought you would be out all day. It's barely lunchtime."

"We need to talk," said Edie, taking a step forward. She glanced back at the painting room and then at her grandmother. The memories of their argument from last night were too bright, too sharp inside her head. She didn't want to go back in there. Not yet. "Can we go to the kitchen? And sit there? I will make you a drink."

"You are not answering my question."

"No," Edie said serenely. "I am not." She paused only to lock the front door of the château behind them before leading her grandmother and Calla and Hanna and Good Sister June into the château kitchen. It was a large, bright room with copper pans hung up against the wall, and a big, long table running all the way down the middle of it. Cupboards were full of tins and boxes, and all of them arranged with the labels face out so that people could instantly see what was where. It was all so neat and clean and *organized* that it made Good Sister June nearly cry with happiness.

"Sit down," said Edie. She gestured at the chairs before grabbing cups from a cupboard and turning on the burner. It had been years since she'd done this but everything was still in the same place. It was as if she'd never been away at all. The chocolate was still in the cupboard and the milk was still kept on the top shelf of the fridge. She began by pouring some milk into a pan and adding a little bit of cinnamon, salt, and sugar. As the milk began to froth and bubble, she broke the chocolate up into smaller pieces and dropped it in the pan. She whisked it all together carefully and then when the mixture turned dark and glossy, she took a spoon from the drawer and tasted it to check that she hadn't lost her skills. And she hadn't. It was just as she remembered it. Perfect.

She could not stop herself from smiling as she poured a small amount into each mug. "The English think they understand hot chocolate, but they do not," she said, as she began to pass them out to the others. "This is hot chocolate. You will understand the difference when you taste it."

Odette raised her finely shaped eyebrows at that. "You came back early to talk about hot chocolate?"

"I came back early to talk with you," said Edie. She sat down and took a deep breath. "We have had such an interesting morning, Grand-Mère. Some of the school went to the Louvre and some of it went to the Marché au Puces de Saint-Ouen. The flea markets, you know? And even though we were in different spaces, something quite unusual happened while we were there. Would you like to know what that was?"

"I feel as if I have no choice."[119]

"We were greeted by your duck," said Edie. "And although ducks cannot talk and they cannot clearly fly across the city to talk to specific groups of people, this one did, and it did so to us."

A disbelieving expression slid across Odette's face. She looked left and then right, as though to try to figure out whether everybody else had just heard what her granddaughter had

---

119   This is accurate. There is very little that can stop a purposeful twelve-year-old.

said. And then, when she saw their expressions, she said, "I feel I must remind you that a duck cannot talk."

Edie gave Calla a prompting look.

"Some of them can," Calla said quietly. "Could, I mean. Maybe. Technically none of the breeds we know *talk* but there's a breed called the Qvada duck and it *used* to exist, and maybe it still exists, and I think that your duck might be it and actually, if it is, then I think it kind of can talk and maybe that it did talk to us."

There was a long and thick silence, the sort of silence that felt packed with words even though nobody was speaking.

And then, in a very resigned sort of voice, Odette said, "If we accept the fact that my duck can speak—which I do not accept remotely, by the way, because It Is a Duck—then the logical question is to ask what it said."

Edie took a long sip of her hot chocolate before she replied. "We shall discuss that in a moment. Before that, though, I want to tell you about what we were doing in the markets and in the Louvre. My friends and I were looking for clues about the painting. Your painting. The one that they keep trying to steal. The theory is that if we can keep it safe, we shall show to you the skills that this school has taught me. And you shall be convinced that you should keep me in it."

"That is ridiculous," said Odette, unable to stop herself. "It is of no use asking me about that painting. There is nothing you can do. And even if there was, why would any of that remotely make me change my mind? That school is not good for you."

"It's the best school I've ever been to," said Hanna. "And I've been to a *lot* of schools."

"I've not been to many schools," said Calla, "but I do know that this school is amazing."[120]

Edie gave them both a little smile. Sometimes a part of her wanted to do things all by herself and walk independently through the world, but then she remembered how much better it felt to do things with Hanna and Calla at her side. It was just like her parents had taught her, all those years ago. When you stood shoulder to shoulder with somebody, you could change the world.

"Are we finished?" Odette said suddenly. She stood up and pushed her chair back, the legs scraping against the tiled floor. "I wish to leave—"

"Tell us about Kurt and Agathe Mercier," said Edie.

---

120 Good Sister June did not say anything. She was too busy having a little moment of pride in her wonderful students.

175

A LIGHT IN THE DARKNESS

Odette's eyes grew wide. Her whole body suddenly started to shake and for a moment it looked like she might faint.

Good Sister June instantly sprang into action.[121] She grabbed Odette in her arms and supported her as she sat back down. "Put your head between your knees and take a deep breath. One after the other. It's all right. Take your time." Odette's breath was ragged, faint, and Good Sister June didn't move until it returned to normal. It was only a few seconds but it felt like forever. She was almost ready to faint herself, when she sat back down.

Silently, Edie rose from her chair and went round the table. She slid her arm across her grandmother's shoulders, pushing the hot chocolate over to her with her free hand. "Drink some of it," she said simply. "I am so sorry, Grand-Mère. I did not mean to startle you like that. I did not know. I am so sorry." She heard Calla and Hanna making similar sounds of apology[122] behind her, but all her interest was on her grandmother. She had never quite realized how small and old she was. It was

---

121 If you imagine an energetic penguin flailing their wings a lot, you will have a good idea what this looked like.

122 "Sorry." "Yes, what she said."

as if she was seeing her for the first time. "I'm sorry," she said again. "Please—take your time. We do not have to have this conversation now. Or ever. I do not want to upset you."

"It does not upset me," Odette said faintly.[123] She slowly sat up, shaking her head as though trying to bring herself back into the moment. A thread of her snow-white hair had escaped from its tight, neat clip and was curling loosely around her neck. Edie had never seen her look like this. Like a person. Like a real and actual person. "I am just—it was a shock. That is all. I just—I never thought—I have not heard those names for a long while. And to hear it so suddenly, here, it was—a shock." She paused and then, with the same delicious honesty that Edie could demonstrate on occasion, added, "But you were not to know that. I have never told you. How could you know?"

Edie didn't move her arm. If anything, she squeezed her grandmother tighter. "I am sorry, though," she said again, before sliding down into the chair next to her. In a strange way, she felt as if this was the first time she had ever met her grandmother. Even the way she was speaking was different.

"We can go," Good Sister June said quietly. "We can wait outside."

Odette looked up. "No," she said, in that strange, soft tone of voice. "I have hidden for long enough. Maybe this is a sign. Maybe it's time for me to tell our story."

---

123 And also bravely, I think.

AND THIS IS THE STORY SHE TOLD

When Odette Berger was born, she was not known by this name. She was called Odette Dupont and she was the sort of baby who was barely alive at all. The operation to save her took from dusk to dawn and halfway through the next day after that. It was only when the sky began to darken on the second day that the doctors told her parents that she would live.

And so she did.

She lived to the edge of the city and all the way back again. She threw herself against everything that the world could give and even though those encounters would often leave her sore and aching, she would get up the next day and do it all over again. Her father, Hugo, tried to lock her in their flat to keep her safe, but she simply climbed out the bedroom window and escaped across the rooftops.[124] Her mother, Emilie, tried to give her chores to distract and occupy her time, but she did them faster than she'd ever expected her to. Odette was so

----

124 Clearly this talent has passed on to the younger members of the Berger family.

determined. Nothing was going to stop her from living her life in the way that she chose.

She would climb the hill of Sacré-Cœur so that she could watch the sunset from the top of it; she would run down the long, shaded avenues of the Tuileries, pausing only to feed the birds and ride the carousel; and then she would walk to the Arc de Triomphe and then down the Champs-Élysées and pretend that she was rich enough to eat at the fine restaurants there; and after all of that, she would return home when it was dark so that she could sleep and do it all over again.

Paris was as big and as full of people then as it is now, but none of them knew it like Odette did. She could tell you the shortcuts from here to there, navigate you across the city in a heartbeat, and stop only to show you the secrets on your own street that you'd never seen before. She was an explorer because she needed to be. She needed to know every inch of it. She couldn't bear the thought of not knowing. The thought of living in that same small flat on the same small street forever left her full of dread. She needed something else. There had to be something else in the world for her, and she searched for it in every inch of the city.

And then, one day, she found it.

She had not intended to visit the Louvre that day, but she did. Her feet took her down to the museum, and there was nothing else she could do but trust them. And so she arrived there on a Friday, the day after she'd turned sixteen years old, and she lined up alongside families with babies in prams, and nannies who would have much rather been somewhere else. She could not afford the entrance fee for any of the places she visited, and so she had become skilled at finding ways to get into them without being discovered. This time, she found twelve girls who had lined up neatly in two little lines behind a nun. She was not the sort of nun who noticed when twelve became thirteen—even when one was much taller than the others. She led them into the museum and then, just as she turned around to check that she had all of her girls still with her, Odette disappeared. She dodged behind a group of tourists and followed a family into one of the wings, and then all of a sudden, she found the thing that she'd been looking for all of her life.

A girl with bright red hair and a smile that could move mountains.

THE BEAUTY OF EVERYTHING

The girl's name was Agathe Mercier.

She was visiting the Louvre with her father, Kurt, and he was teaching her how to be an artist. Odette found herself following them through the museum, and every word they shared made her future open up more and more. They would talk about light and color and shade, and the way they referred to the people in the paintings made her realize that they were actually real people for the first time in her life. That behind the stillness and the severe expressions on the canvas were people living real lives in real houses, just like hers.

It made her feel feverish. She was hot and cold and full and empty all at once. The only thing she knew was that she had been looking for something else all her life, something more than the struggling and sad existence that she was destined to have, and that day the world gave it to her.

In a way, I think that Kurt Mercier realized all of this. He was somebody who saw the world around him in detail, and he saw Odette in a way that nobody else had ever done. That's why he walked so slowly through that museum and why he talked so loudly about the paintings that they stood in front of. He was teaching her as much as Agathe. They continued like this for an hour or two, the three of them walking through the museum together, until he turned to Odette and looked her straight in the eye. "You cannot hear anything from such a distance," he said. "Come closer, if you please. I do not lecture to the room, but only to those I choose. And I choose you as much as my daughter. I see it in you. You want to know more."

Odette stared at him. She had followed many people through the city, trailing their shadows down the avenues and boulevards[125] and she had imagined a thousand lives and destinies for them as she did so. Not one of them had ever noticed her, let alone talked to her.

But none of those people had been Kurt Mercier. He had spent his whole life looking for the details that other people missed, so when Odette still did not say anything, he took her to the side of the room and pressed a pencil and notebook into her hands. "I want to try something with you," he said in his firm, big voice. "I want you to draw something. Anything. Do not think about it."

Inevitably, she did not know what to do. Her mind filled with a thousand thoughts and feelings, all at once, and her hand froze into stillness. She couldn't move. She couldn't even think clearly. A part of her wanted to give Kurt his pencil back and run out of the museum. The only thing that was

----

125 And once, past a flower shop on the Rue de la Vérité, where a very young Madame Clement was playing outside of a shop and dreaming about owning it.

stopping her was the thought of never seeing the girl with the red hair again. She wanted to look at her forever.

Kurt smiled. "One of my teachers at the Staatliches Bauhaus, a marvelous man,[126] once told me that drawing was nothing more than taking a line for a walk. The authorities in my country, now, they hate his art, but I think he is perhaps the most brilliant artist I have ever known. So! My point is this, girl: Take your pencil for a walk and see what happens. It is not too much to ask, I think. And I would not ask it of you if I did not think you could do it."

And then the girl with the red hair spoke. "It's easier than you think," she said.

Five words. Five words to have Odette's heart completely.

That was all it took.

---

126 Kurt is talking about an artist called Paul Klee here, who I am Very Fond Of. You should look him up on the internet when you have finished reading this book. Normally I would do some research and suggest a link or two for you to follow, but Good Sister Gwendolyn is on Netflix again and using up all our bandwidth, so I have had a custard cream instead.

THE SHADOW THAT FORMED

That drawing was not good. It was barely even a drawing. She just scrawled something with her eyes half closed and gave it back to him in the hope that it would suit. It was not a drawing of anything and yet, it was enough to change her life.

Kurt saw something in it and Odette that made him decide to hire her as a companion[127] to Agathe. She was to go back with them to Munich and study alongside her in the hope of—perhaps—one day becoming an artist.[128] He promised to teach her everything that he taught his own daughter, and even if Odette did not become an artist, she would be able to teach people or work at the museum herself. It was a career, a life.

....

127 This is a fancy word for somebody who is friends with a person and looks after them.

128 "I never even knew that you had left the country," Edie said wonderingly. "I thought you did not even know where the edge of the world was. A part of me was convinced that you thought everywhere was France. Like Poland was France but with more snow, and England was France but with substantially more depressing breakfasts."

Odette smiled. "France is the best, yes, of course. But there's a benefit to be found in travel. You understand what you have. You realize what matters to you. You realize how ready you are to fight for it."

It was hope in a world that had long since decided not to give her any of it.

Her parents did not believe what had happened to her that day, and it took a long while for them to be convinced. It was the late 1930s, and Europe was starting to slide slowly toward a war that nobody wanted. The thought of sending their daughter to another country in the middle of all of that was almost too much for Emilie and Hugo Dupont to think of. But slowly Kurt convinced them. He told them about how it would give Odette a future. An income. Money to help her make a better life. And while he told them of this, Odette herself sat outside with Agathe and wondered how to tell her that she loved her.

It is not often that people fall in love like that, but Agathe and Odette did. They made sense together. For Odette, it was like finding a part of herself that she hadn't even known was missing. When she found the words to talk, she barely needed them. All she needed to do was smile at Agathe and for her to smile back. That was it.

That was all of it.

A BRIEF FLICKER OF SUNLIGHT

And so to Munich. It was a city that was the headquarters of the Nazis, and the streets were full of uniformed soldiers and members of their party. There were parades regularly in the streets that proclaimed the might and strength of the German nation, and the radio played nothing but propaganda and yet, even in the middle all of that madness and horror, Kurt and Agathe and Odette found joy. They lived from day to day like bohemians with nothing to do in the world but appreciate beauty and life itself. Whenever one of Kurt's friends threw a party, they would go and drink and eat and listen to ideas that might change the world, or if they heard about somebody doing some interesting work at the far side of the city, then the three of them would take a tram to somewhere they'd never before been to, just to try to see what was happening. If they wanted to eat breakfast in the middle of the night or to wear dressing gowns in the middle of the day, then they would. Odette loved it. She had spent so long being told to be scared of the world that she had never quite realized how much it all had to give her.

And then, one day, she realized how much it could take away.

THE LIGHT THAT WENT OUT

Kurt Mercier was killed.

He was killed underneath a bright blue sky and a sun so fine and clear that it might have been shaped from gold. It was not the sort of day to die in, and he had not expected to die. He had been waiting for Agathe and Odette to return home from their classes at university, and he had prepared a supper of some bread and some cheese, and then he had answered the door to some Nazi soldiers and everything had changed.

He had expected this visit for a while, for the things he painted made him visible in a world where it paid to be the very opposite. And so when these soldiers arrived at the flat, Kurt let them in and listened to what they had to say. He had no choice. The soldiers told him he was saying the wrong sorts of things and painting the wrong sorts of people. They mentioned one painting in particular that had offended them: a painting of two young women with their arms around each other and seemingly in love. Kurt changed the subject quickly at this point, but the soldiers did not. They told him that his art was degenerate.[129] If he continued to make art in the way

....

129   This was a word that the Nazis used to describe the art that they did not

that he wanted to, then they would make it so that he could not buy canvases or paint or anything to work with. They would prevent him from selling his art and from lecturing at the university.

Once they had told him this, they told him that he could stop it from happening. He must never paint again unless it was in the way that they wanted him to. Munich was to be a capital of art, but only the sort of art that was right and proper to produce. Art that shared the values of the Nazis and all that they stood for. Kurt could keep painting if only he painted the right things. Other artists had agreed to this. They told him about the artist who now only painted innocent views of the countryside, and about the man who had handed in his oil paintings without complaint. It was all very straightforward. All Kurt had to do was paint what they told him or stop. There was nothing more to it.

Kurt told them that he would not stop painting.

That he would continue to paint precisely what he wanted and how he wanted.

And so they shot him.

....

agree with. For them, art had to show the way that they wanted the world to be and what they wanted it to look like. Kurt's big and bright paintings, full of heart and love and life, were something that they hated very much.

THERE IS NO SHAME IN SADNESS

It was here that Odette stopped for the first time since she had begun her story and looked at the people opposite her. "The one thing that you must know is that it is worth crying for the people or the things that you love. You must never be ashamed of it. And the love I hold for that brave and wonderful man is something I shall never be ashamed of."

Edie pulled her chair so close to Odette that they were almost touching. "You do not have to continue if you do not wish to," she said. "Please—you do not have to do this."

"But I do," said Odette. "I have been waiting years to tell you this. And at last, I've begun. I will not stop."

NEVERTHELESS, THEY RESISTED

Odette and Agathe joined the Resistance the day after Kurt was murdered.

It sounds so straightforward and yet that was the last thing on earth that it was.

Being a member of the Resistance meant that they could not trust anybody but each other. They would distribute the leaflets and posters that they were given, sticking them up across the college in the middle of the still and silent night, but they never knew who printed them nor how they arrived at the apartment. The packages would be slid underneath their door in the early hours of the morning and neither Odette nor Agathe wanted to open it and see who was on the other side. Some things were better not knowing.

After a while, the two girls also began to get messages sent to them. They would be in the university library, studying one of the few books that had not been burned, when a note would appear in one of their pockets. Somebody asking for help in hiding paintings from a gallery that was about to be ransacked. Somebody else needing help to get to the station before the soldiers came knocking at their door. Odette and

Agathe would talk about these requests in the middle of the night, their heads almost touching in their bed and their voices no louder than a whisper, before one of them got out to burn the note. And then, in the morning, they would gather their courage to them and go off and help whoever needed them.

It was not easy. The soldiers had the flat marked as somewhere to watch and so they did. They would stand on the opposite side of the street for hours, just waiting for one of the girls to do something that they could imprison her for. They would quiz the people in the flats above and below to try to find some evidence of a crime. Did they ever smell oil paints being used?[130] Did Agathe and Odette talk to anybody that they shouldn't? Was there anything happening that the authorities should know about?

None of these questions could ever be answered in the way that the Nazis wanted them to be, for Odette and Agathe were too smart for that. They forced themselves to pick up part-time jobs in shops owned by families who had been accepted by the Nazis and all that their awful regime stood for. They went to church on a Sunday and stood next to soldiers and government officials and, even though it broke their hearts, smiled at them after the service and wished them well. And

----

130 This question might not make much sense to you, so let me explain. Oil paints were something that Kurt had used in his paintings, and people could smell them from the flats above and below. If they were being used in the flat after he had died, that meant that the girls had been painting—just as Kurt had—and that meant that the soldiers could come into the flat and "talk" to them—just as they had with Kurt.

whenever the lies and the fear grew too much for the two of them to handle, they would think about how they had not yet been able to clean out Kurt's room or even sit in his chair at the table, and whenever that was not enough, they would hold each other very tightly in the dead of night and remember that they were in love and that nobody would ever take that away from them.

UNTIL THAT FINAL DAY

It began like every other day that they had spent together. They distributed a thousand leaflets that morning, working quickly in the fine gray mist of the dawn, and the adrenaline from that had kept them going all day. They kept reliving every breathless step that they'd taken, telling their stories of near-misses and close calls in the quietest and softest of whispers, knowing that the walls were thin and their neighbors a threat.

But then the knock on the door came. Two knocks, to be precise. Whoever it was knocked long enough to be deliberate, long enough to be noticed by the two girls inside the flat, and yet still somehow short enough for them to disappear by the time that Odette threw open the door.

The only thing that she saw was a small piece of paper on the mat.

It had one word on it. Just one.

Run.

RUN, RUN, AS FAST AS YOU CAN

And so the two of them ran.

They left their toast uneaten on the kitchen counter, and they threw everything that mattered to them into one big bag. Their passports and papers; all of the things that would let them leave Germany and enter France. All of the money that the two of them had in the world. A photograph of Kurt in a silver frame. And a painting—just the one—rolled up tight inside a protective tube. It was a portrait of the two of them. Kurt had painted Odette and Agathe together. He had insisted on doing it and it had been a dangerous thing to do, for it showed the girls with their arms around each other and love in their eyes, but he could not stop himself. And the painting was good because of it. Everybody who saw it knew it was the best thing Kurt had ever done. And the most dangerous.

Agathe and Odette took the painting and their money and they ran. They left the apartment and headed off down the street in the middle of the night. They dodged the eyes of everyone who might have looked at them and walked in the shadows that were far away from the bright glare of the street-lights. When a car came too close, or drove past too slowly,

Odette pulled up the collar of her coat and Agathe looked down at the ground so that her hair swung forward to hide her face.[131]

At first neither of them knew where they were going. They just knew they had to be somewhere else before the soldiers came to the flat, and so they made themselves disappear, just like the people they'd spent the past few weeks helping.

"There is a train leaving in a couple of hours," said Agathe. She was breathing heavily, like somebody who'd just finished a race. She was flushed with color and her hair had begun to curl in the damp dawn mist. "A morning one—it goes all the way to Paris. It's the same route we used when you came back with us. As long as the line's not been bombed, you'll be able to make it. You'll be able to get on board and buy a ticket there[132]—"

On a better day, Odette would have recognized that there was something wrong. She would have realized how carefully Agathe was telling her this. She would have noticed the detail that was missing and the things that she was not saying, but she did not. She was too far gone with nerves and fears to realize anything but the hope of escape. And so she nodded and agreed and the two of them began to walk toward the station. They were lucky that it was so early. People do not see much

---

131 "Holy Harriet the Spy," whispered Hanna. Her eyes were wide and disbelieving. "I did not expect any of this."

132 You might be wondering how I know all this, so here is where I tell you how I do. Sometimes we have conversations in our lives that we never forget and this was one of mine with Odette. And telling it to the girls that day in the kitchen was one of the bravest things I have ever seen.

when it is early, and the things that they do see, they are too tired to take note of. Two young girls were nothing unusual. They were shaking and pale, but again that was not unusual in a city that was already desperate with hunger. You only saw the people who did not shake, who marched down the streets as if they owned them.

They got to the train. Somehow they managed to get tickets, somehow they beat the last-minute rush of people who appeared from nowhere, somehow they found two seats together in a far corner of a quiet carriage, and somehow neither of them cried with relief when the train left the station and began to work its way toward the borders and toward freedom.

But only one of them would ever see it.

IN WHICH WE PAUSE

"I am not stopping," Odette said faintly. "Just pausing. There is a very precise difference. I have not told anybody any of this for many years. A part of me thought that I never would. It hurt too much to even begin. It still hurts but now, perhaps I think, it hurts in a different way."

Edie leaned forward and took her grandmother's hands in her own. "Let us hurt for you," she said. "Be afraid of this pain no longer. We will bear it for you. Please. If you can. Tell us what happened next."

And so Odette did.

THE END OF THE LINE

The train stopped at the border.

It did not move for a very long time.

It was meant to move, of course. It should have stopped for people to have their passports and papers checked, but that should have just been for a few minutes. The two girls should have been in Paris by the end of the day and safe.

But the train stopped.

Odette began to grow worried. She felt it deep inside of her bones and she was not the only one. All of the other passengers realized it as well. Those who were old and tired closed their eyes and dreamt of a world without borders and sadness. Those who were still full of fight and hope began to talk and try to figure out what to do. Some of them passed belongings and children between them, gently hiding sleeping babies inside of suitcases and giving toddlers to strangers, in the hope that some fragment of their life might survive that which was to come. And a few of the bravest, or perhaps the most foolish, began to put their coats on and inch toward the train door. France was so close. They could run for it. Only barbed wire and a checkpoint stood between it and them.

A part of Odette wanted to run for it as well, but she did not. She sat there and told herself that there was nothing to be afraid of. She told herself that there was a war on, that the line might have been bombed, and that nobody knew that she and Agathe were on the train. They had left so suddenly and so sharply that nobody would know that they were here. Within hours, they would be in Paris and safe.

She tried to distract herself by looking around the carriage and noticing the people about her. Kurt had taught her that looking at the world mattered, and so she did. One of the first things she saw was a man. He was sitting slightly apart from everyone else and didn't seem to have realized what was happening. He hadn't even looked up from his book.

But she could tell that he had noticed everything. He was holding himself very precisely together, watching the people in the carriage, and seeing it all out of the corner of his eye. Occasionally his fingers would tap the pile of packages he had on his lap, all of them wrapped in brown paper and tied firmly together with string. As she watched him, he undid a knot and then redid it within seconds, his fingers moving almost on instinct.

And then Agathe grabbed her hand.

A cloud of soldiers had entered the carriage. There were so many of them pressed together in their dark uniforms that it felt like they were a flock of crows, blocking out the sun and the sky. They were checking everybody's passports and papers. Every now and then they would pause and surround some poor soul before taking them off the train. Those people didn't even have time to look back. They were marched away and within seconds, gone.

Odette squeezed Agathe's hand. It was instinctive. She told herself that they would survive it. That the two of them would live their lives together and grow old.

But then Agathe whispered something into Odette's ear.

And the whole world went silent.

WHAT AGATHE SAID

"I'm going to give myself up," she whispered. "You're French. You've got a chance. I'm German, and the daughter of a painter who they hated. Who they killed. And that means that I can distract them long enough for you to run. And you must. You *will*. You will do this for me. Because I love you. Because one of us has to survive."

LIVING FOR THE ONES YOU LOVE

Odette paused here. "I have lived that moment a thousand times. Her words in my ear. My heart beating loud enough to wake the dead. And I have never been able to stop what happened next. Agathe stood up from her seat. She paused only to rearrange her hair and neaten her coat, before making her way down the carriage to meet her fate head-on. The bravery of it. She was astounding."

There was silence in the kitchen. Edie had not moved from Odette's side. Hanna and Calla were barely breathing. And Good Sister June was trying very hard to not cry into the last bits of her hot chocolate.

After a while, Odette nodded as if she had come to a decision. "Yes," she said. "I shall tell you what happened next. For her, I shall tell you it all."

HOW TO SAVE A LIFE

It happened as Agathe reached the soldiers. A man produced his gun instead of his passport and suddenly the whole carriage exploded with panic. Somebody started to scream; the people who'd been stood at the door seized the moment to force it open and run down the side of the station platform; somebody else attacked the soldier who was standing nearest to him in the hopes of overpowering him. Guns suddenly burst into life from all corners of the carriage, firing at the soldiers, who dropped to their knees and began to fire back. Some passengers smashed the windows and climbed out of their carriage. Those who were already bleeding or trapped by the panicked crowd of passengers pushed their children through the broken glass and told them to run for the border and not look back. The old woman sitting opposite Odette began to haul her out of her seat and shove her toward the door. Odette tried to turn back and fight her way to Agathe, but the sudden press of people behind her was too solid. She was carried out of the train and onto the platform before she quite realized what was happening.

As the crowd broke around her and ran for the French border, a whole host of soldiers suddenly appeared out of nowhere to hold them back. Amid the screams and the shouts and the gunshots, Odette turned back to the carriage to look for Agathe. She was near the far door, visible despite the mess of people and smoke due to the bright color of her hair, and Odette watched her push and fight her way through the crowds of people who were still on the train. Instinctively Odette ran forward, dodging the sound of bullets as they cracked loudly over her head, and somehow managed to get to the side of the carriage. She smashed one of the windows open with her elbow and yelled for Agathe, who somehow heard her and turned. The two of them locked eyes. Agathe took a swift and sudden step toward her. Odette reached out. Their fingers brushed.

And then the bullet hit Agathe.

Her eyes went wide.
For a moment she looked more alive than Odette
had ever seen her.
And then she fell.

HOW TO BEGIN AGAIN

"I don't know how long I stood there," said Odette. She wrapped her hands around her hot chocolate, even though it had long since grown cold. "I was waiting, I think, for somebody to tell me that it had not happened, that I had dreamt it all, but they never did. And so eventually, I moved. I picked up one foot after another and I made for the border. Or rather, I headed toward what remained of it."

MY NAME IS ODETTE

The borders between countries can be quite strange places indeed. There is a house, for example, that sits right on the border of the United States of America, with the front door in that country and the back door in Canada. Another house sits right on the border between the Netherlands and Belgium, where you can have breakfast in one country and your supper in the next.

Not all borders are marked in this gentle way. The border that Odette had reached was one full of knotted, twisted wire and the station was right in the middle of it. The tracks led into France but they were unreachable due to the riot of people pouring out of the train in a desperate search for freedom. And also the soldiers. They had raced out of the station buildings and over to the train, some of them dropping to their knees and shooting anybody who dared run down the tracks, whilst others were climbing on the train to deal with what was happening there.

The only option to get through the border was at a small checkpoint in the middle of the fence. It was enough for a single truck to get through and no more. It had a barrier across it that had been lowered in an attempt to stop people pushing their way past. In front of it stood a soldier with his gun pointing at the riot of passengers that surged toward him. He ordered them back several times and then when that did not work, he shot at those people who were nearest and stole their lives from them without a moment's hesitation. Some people turned back toward the train then and tried to find somewhere else to run, but others pushed forward. One man, the same man that Odette had noticed on the train, was right at the front of the crowd. His hand was full of a roll of banknotes, his smile wide, and his eyes bright. He began to offer money to the soldier and asked him to move away from the barrier.

It was when she saw something move out of the corner of her eye, Odette realized why the man was doing this. There was a group of girls, maybe ten or eleven years old, who had found a gap in the fence just behind the soldier and were trying to get through. They looked exhausted. They were covered in dust and shattered glass from the windows on the train. One of them was bleeding, another limping, and the third—the tallest of them—had her arms wrapped tightly around a silent and stunned baby. There was no sign of an adult anywhere. As Odette watched them, she saw the limping girl start to carefully help the others through the so-small gap in the fence. If the soldier saw any of this, the girls would be shot. The man was trying to distract him. He was trying to save their lives.

Odette stepped forward and took the man's hand in hers. When he looked at her with a quick, uncomprehending stare, she squeezed it and turned to the soldier. "Do you not know who this man is?" She said it in French first and then German, and her voice was calm and still, as if she was in the middle of a storm and untouched by either rain or wind. "Have you even looked at him? He is an important man in the French government. He works in Paris at the—" Here she invented a government department, something long and complicated and furiously fictional. It did not matter what its name was. It just had to sound right. She had learned so much about how to manage these monstrous men over the past few weeks. "If there's a reason you're delaying him, people will need to know. I am from Munich, myself. I know many people there, and all of them value what this man does for them. Do you want to tell me why you're delaying him? And all of his friends? I will have to report back to my superiors. What is your name? Let me make sure I tell them everything—"

In the distance, she saw the final girl slide under the fence and make her way to freedom. The man at her side saw it too and squeezed her hand back, suddenly understanding what she was doing and willing her on. And so she continued. She mentioned the names of all the important people in Munich, all of the people she had forced herself to serve in the shop and sit next to in church, and when she felt herself running out of names and breath, Odette decided that she only had one option left.

So she punched him.

LIBERTY

As the soldier fell heavily to the ground, a roar of relief erupted from the crowd. Everybody began to push forward and into France, pausing only to thank Odette as they passed. The old woman who'd pulled Odette off the train was one of the last to cross the border. Her clothes were smeared with dirt from where she'd fallen, but somebody had helped her up and another person had their arms around her now and was helping her to walk. She paused only to kiss Odette before walking slowly and steadily away into the distance.

The man at Odette's side said, "We have to go now. That soldier's not going to be happy when he wakes up. We don't want to be here for that."

Odette took a long moment to reply. She felt a little bit as if she was gathering all of the parts of herself together again after they'd been blown apart. "I don't know your name."

"My name is Luc Berger," he replied. "You were right, by the way. I do work for the government. How could you tell?"

"I see a lot," she said. "Too much, perhaps. It's my gift."

He looked at her. "Who *are* you?"

"I don't know anymore," said Odette. Her entire life had been on that train. She had lost it all. There was nothing left. "But I have to get to Paris. Will you help me?"

Luc nodded. "Always."

KEEPING YOUR HEAD
ABOVE THE WATER

There are moments in the world that change the people that we are and the life that we lead. Odette's life had changed when she met Agathe, and it had changed all over again when she had watched Agathe die, and the Odette who finally made her way back into Paris to fall into the arms of her parents was not the one who had left. Her father found himself leaving the windows of the flat open in the hope that Odette would climb out onto the roof in the middle of the night again and he'd have to beg her to come down and back into the flat. Her mother began to invent jobs that needed doing about the house and crossed her fingers that Odette would refuse them all and storm out of the front door, just as she once had when she was young. But she didn't. Odette did everything that Emilie asked her to do and when she went to bed, she closed the windows that Hugo had left open, and she tried to understand how she could go from feeling so much to feeling nothing at all.

Emilie began to receive advice from their neighbors about what she should do with her lost and broken daughter. Old Madame Angier, a ninety-seven-year-old force of nature who lived on a diet of gossip and raw eggs, said that she should make Odette take cold baths first thing in a morning. Their downstairs neighbor, the similarly ancient Monsieur Escoffier, disagreed with her, for he had long ago decided to disagree with Madame Angier on all things. He said that Emilie should lay lavender underneath Odette's pillow to help her sleep and make her eat a freshly boiled egg every day at twelve o'clock. Monsieur and Madame Marchand, who lived in the ground-floor flat and did not like to be left out of any promising gossip, offered an entirely different suggestion. Their belief was that Odette should drink a full glass of milk before she went to bed, and place a slice of ginger to rest on her forehead to calm her thoughts.[133]

It will not surprise you to learn that none of these suggestions worked. Time was the only thing that would heal Odette and she did not have enough of it. The war was about to arrive on her doorstep. France had surrendered, their army had been defeated, and nothing would ever be the same again. Just before the Nazis had entered the city, Monsieur Escoffier and Madame Angier shared a tearful farewell with each other when their families took them out of the city in search of safety. Madame Angier sat in silence as the car pulled off and her thin and freckled hands shook even though she tried to hide them. Monsieur Escoffier's family took him in the opposite direction, somehow finding space for him on the back of a wagon that was already piled high with furniture and

---

[133] The fact that Monsieur and Madame Marchand ran the nearest shop that supplied both of these items was not at all related.

children. Hugo, Emilie, and Odette watched him to the edge of the street, before they lost him in the great crowd of people who were leaving the city as well.

Monsieur and Madame Marchand decided to stay in the city to look after their shop. Emilie and Hugo, who could rather imagine flying than leaving the city they'd known all their life, decided to stay as well. But Odette did not. She had been so visible in Munich, going to church and living her life under the eyes of the Nazis, that there was the risk of somebody recognizing her. And even if they didn't, everybody in their neighborhood knew about her fairy-tale meeting with Kurt and Agathe and her trip to Germany. Anybody would start to wonder what had happened there and when they started to wonder about that, they might figure out who it was who had plastered the university with leaflets and posters against the Nazis, and who it was who had helped all those people disappear, and who had survived the gunfight on the train at the border. Odette could see her life toppling, and in the middle of it: her parents. They were so slender and fragile already. She would not bring the soldiers to their door. She would do everything she could to prevent that.

And so, one day, Odette kissed her parents and told them that she loved them and left. She walked out of that flat and began to make her way through the city that she had known all her life. She walked past cinemas that were changing their signs from French into German, smiled politely at the soldiers already sitting outside cafés, and gave directions to those who could not understand the French street signs. She dodged the checkpoints by cutting through the front door of one café and out of the back of another; she crossed the Seine twice, doubling back to check that she hadn't been followed, before she finally headed down a street called the Rue de la Vérité.[134] At the end of this street was a long path that headed up a hill and to a château that overlooked the city.

Odette walked up the hill and to the front door of the château. She knocked firmly on it three times.

The door opened. A man looked out.

His eyes widened with recognition.

"Hello, Luc Berger," said Odette. "Will you help me once more?"

---

134 Sound familiar?

WHAT LUC BERGER DID

Luc Berger hid Odette, and he did so in plain sight. He worked in the government in an office with an unpronounceable name and an even more unpronounceable purpose, and it meant that he had enough power to invent a sudden need for a secretary and for that to be Odette. She became Odette Leroux, a woman with impeccable credentials and a background that was sadly unable to be checked due to the bombing of her home and all that it contained. Luc gave her somewhere to stay and also helped to forge her new papers in the middle of the night. They labored by candlelight, the two of them barely breathing as they put together the papers that would keep her safe.

The papers succeeded. Luc and Odette worked quietly and calmly together, and used every opportunity that they had to pass information to the Resistance. When they were sent to the big warehouses on the edge of the city, full of confiscated belongings and things that the Nazis had stolen, they began to make lists of where the objects had come from. Although they longed to give the objects back, they could not do so. That was simply too dangerous for everybody concerned, and so they began to make lists instead. They recorded everything that they came across and where it had come from and where it was going. They recorded the destination of the train that it was put on, noted down the details of the officers who selected them for their homes, and spent their nights testing each other on the detail. Odette's training as an artist made her able to remember everything. Luc could never keep up with his notes, and he would constantly have to ask her to slow down and repeat herself. And when they were finished, they hid the lists behind loose stones in the chimney, and sometimes they'd wrap them up in gabardine[135] and tuck them behind the gargoyles up on the roof.

One day they were sent to a warehouse they hadn't been to before. Within seconds, they realized why. This was for the things that nobody wanted to look at. Luggage had been pulled from burning houses, the smoke and scorch of flames still fresh upon them, and the great pile of empty shoes in the corner of the building made Odette go outside and throw up. She was joined within seconds by Luc, tears streaming from his eyes, and it was only the presence of several Nazi soldiers working outside the building that made the two of them go back inside.

And that was when they found the painting.

It was in a pile of bullet-riddled papers; the top was a photograph of a young family that Odette had made herself look at and commit to memory, and then, as she began to flick through the rest of the pile she suddenly saw herself and

----

135 This is a fancy word for a kind of material that is waterproof.

Agathe looking back at her. The painting. It was stained now and torn but still whole enough to make her heart stop with recognition and her whole body start to shake. Her hand shook. She said, "Luc—" and then she couldn't say anything else and just gestured at the painting.

He glanced at her. "That's you," he said, almost unnecessarily.

She nodded.

"Is it yours? Do you own it?"

She nodded.

Luc glanced around. They were alone. He took a swift step forward. He picked up the painting. He slid it into the inside of his jacket.

And as simple as that, it was hers again.

TOGETHERNESS

"That was the day I realized that he loved me," said Odette softly. "He didn't ask me about who the other person was. Or why I wanted it. He just knew that I needed it and so he took it. If they had found him with it, they would have killed him. But they didn't. He wouldn't have let them. And so, at last, I had a memory of the woman I loved and I have never let it leave my side since. I named you after her, Edie, do you know that?"

"I never knew," Edie replied blankly.

"Nobody knew about Agathe," said Odette. "Luc never asked. He was a good man. He knew that she was important to me, and that was all he needed to risk his life for it. I've never told anybody about her but when you were born, I was insistent. You had to have her name. I had lost my name by then. Odette Dupont was nothing but a dream, but you were not. Edmée Agathe Aurore Berger. Looking at you was like looking at her. Even from the day you were born. You remind me so much of her. I could love you in one breath and be terrified of losing you in the other. I knew what this city—what this world could do to the things I loved."

And because Edie had begun to understand her strange and proud grand-mère in a way that she had never thought possible, she pressed her hands tightly around hers. "Will you show us the painting? I would like to see it now that I understand it. I do not think I ever saw it clearly before."[136]

"No," said Odette, agreeing. "I think that, perhaps, I did not understand the painting. The fault is all mine."[137] She glanced over at Calla and Hanna and Good Sister June. "Will you come with us to the painting room? I would like you all to see it, now that you know about who painted it and who the other girl is."

"Yes," said Calla. "Of course. Thank you."

"We would be honored," said Good Sister June.

The five of them walked slowly out of the kitchen and toward the front of the château. Edie could not quite believe how quickly her world had changed and yet, now that it had, she could not imagine anything better. Her grand-mère was, at last, making sense to her.

"After you," said Edie when they reached the door of the painting room. "I think you should go in first."

"Thank you, Edie," said Odette and then, suddenly, she stopped.

Because the painting was gone.

---

136 In a way, I do not think that she was talking about the painting at all here.

137 And in a way, Odette was not talking about the painting either.

AND WHEN THEY GOT THERE, THE CUPBOARD WAS BARE

Dear Madame Berger and those girls and also to that woman who dresses a bit like a penguin, you are all MOST annoying. This is not usually the sort of thing I leave when I steal something but honestly, you are the WORST.[138] *I thought you had gone out for the day and that nobody was left in the building but then some of you came back. Who does that? What sort of people can see Paris in a morning? I had to hide under the sofa when Madame Berger came in, and THEN I had to order a delivery of chocolate éclairs to distract the nuns upstairs and after that, I had to order an emergency pack of biscuits for those hideous hounds and that duck (let me tell you this, texting when you are under a sofa is QUITE HARD), and then when you all came back early anyway, I thought that it was all over. But it wasn't! You all went off to the kitchens! So HELPFUL. Thank you! All I have wanted to do is remove this painting*

---

138   I suspect in his eyes, we were just as bad as a chocolate cake with Unexpected Jam inside.

*from your house and at last I've been able to do so. I will
give you an excellent review on châteauxtostealfrom
.com, I promise.*[139] *(You will see that I have left the frame
for you to dispose of yourself. My client only wanted
the canvas. And now they have it!!!) Anyway. That is
enough from me! Goodbye!*

---

139 I have just looked it up and we received an 8.5. Positive points were
"location, accessibility, and also excellent biscuits in the biscuit tub."
Negative points were "the duck ☹, the dogs ☹☹☹, and the persistently
present small girls ☹☹☹."

(In other news, I hope you are impressed that I have learned how to
do smiley faces on the keyboard. It has been a very exciting day and I am
going to have a slice of lemon drizzle to celebrate.)

WHAT TO DO IN AN EXTRAORDINARY SITUATION

There are many things that one can do in such an extraordinary situation. Odette did the best thing that she could have done, which was to cry her heart out with the sheer shock of it all and then collapse into the nearest chair. Edie wrapped a blanket over her shoulders and hugged her deeply before leading the others out of the room. She looked at Good Sister June and then back at the closed door. "Will you stay with her? I do not want her to be alone right now."

Good Sister June nodded. "Of course," she said. "Good Sister Gwendolyn is still around somewhere too, I think. I will get her to come and join us."

"I will phone the police while you do that," said Edie. "Even though they will not be able to solve this crime before us, they should be aware of what has happened."

"And what's going to happen after you finish talking to them?" asked Good Sister June.

Edie looked at her, most innocent. "But why on *earth* do you think that there is something after that?"

"Because I know you all," said Good Sister June. She glanced at Calla and Hanna, who had similarly innocent expressions on their faces. "And you all have the sort of expressions that tell me that Something Is Afoot and I have learned that it is wise to pay attention when that sort of thing happens."[140]

"Oh, Good Sister June, you really are *very* good at adulting," Edie said appreciatively. "Of course we have a plan. But before that—tell me this. When we arrived, did you see other cars or transport outside? Other than our taxi itself?"

Good Sister June shook her head.

"Precisely!" said Edie. Every now and then she really found it quite traumatic how long it could take people to catch up. The only thing that kept her going was the sense of satisfaction she felt when they finally did.[141] "So that means that our culprit is on foot. And that means that he is carrying the painting and there is only one unsecured entrance to the estate, which means that he has not gone far, and so I know precisely where he is. He is on the path that leads to the Rue de la Vérité, the very same path I and my dear parents walked up every Sunday."

"Also, he's not going to be moving quickly," said Hanna, who had been thinking about this ever since she'd seen that awful space on the wall where the painting should have been. "He's taken *Les Roses Blanches* out of the frame and that makes it fragile. He'll have to wrap it up carefully the moment that he can."

"And I don't think he's got anybody helping him," said Calla, who had been similarly putting two and two together and

---

140 Trust me, it just makes it easier in the long run.
141 Because this meant that they had recognized her genius.

making four. "He kept referring to what *he'd* done, and what *his* client wanted—not what anybody else wanted. And even without that, he was by himself when we met him and he was by himself now. It's just him, I'm sure of it."

Edie nodded. "I agree with all of this, my wise and learned acquaintances. Good Sister June, please stay here and look after my dear grand-mère. If she asks where we are, distract her with Adult Matters. We will be back as soon as we can be. Also, could you perhaps go into the kitchen and make us some sandwiches for our return? Ham and cheese for myself, but I leave the rest up to you. Oh! Also! I need you to make two phone calls for me. I will detail who and what in mere moments, but all you need to know now is this one thing.

"We are going to steal that painting back."

PRECISELY WHAT THEY DID

As Calla and Hanna and Edie ran out of the house and down toward the city, Good Sister June made the phone calls that she had been told to make. The first call was to Good Sister Christine, who was currently enjoying a rather splendid afternoon tea at the Tuileries with a substantial portion of the school.[142] The second was to a man called Gareth who was, technically, in prison but also a person who was a Good Chap at Heart and very knowledgeable about certain things.[143] And once she had made these calls, Good Sister June rummaged in the cupboards and made a cup of tea and a sandwich for Odette and herself. A part of her was not quite sure that this was the right thing to do under the circumstances but a bigger part of

---

142 "Hello, I appreciate this is short notice but I need you to send back to the château the following girls: Eloise and Claire Taylor, Lucy Millais, Rose Bastable, Emily Redmond, Maisie Holloway, Sabia and Sethi Gopal, Thea de Grazie, Stine and Greta Dunn, somebody who's got good lock-picking skills, and also some of those really excellent macarons from that shop on the Champs-Élysées."

143 "Gareth, how long would you need to package up a potentially priceless painting for transport and what materials, precisely, would you need to do it? Also, how *is* your ganache going?"

her knew that Edie, Hanna, and Calla could be unstoppable. And so she tried to tell herself to believe that part, even as her cup of tea remained untouched and the sandwich uneaten.

"Good Sister June will be wondering if she has done the right thing," Edie said thoughtfully, as she led the other two girls through the garden. "She would not normally be like this, but I think that she will have been influenced by my grand-mère. Of course, they are both very old[144] and so I suppose we must simply realize that they have no other choice. Really, being an adult just seems *so* dull."[145]

"But I think being like that has nothing to do with whether you're old or not," replied Hanna, jogging alongside her. "I think it's because you choose to be like that that you are like that. I have met *many* people at the embassy who are precisely as exciting as a spoon—"

"Duck," said Edie suddenly.

Calla wrinkled her nose. "I've heard of a lot of ducks, but I've never heard of a spoon duck."

"You are adorable," said Edie. "But right now, I would very much like you to duck."

For they had just come across the remarkable sight of a very small nun firing tranquilizer darts at an art thief.

---

144 Just for the record, Good Sister June was barely into her seventies and not, as Edie may suspect, into her seven hundred and seventies.

145 She is not wrong.

IN WHICH THE COVERT-SKILLS CLASS EXPANDS THEIR CURRICULUM

A brief explanation.

Good Sister Gwendolyn's covert-skills classes had been going excellently well. It was not the sort of class that you could mark in a conventional manner, for things like homework and tests cannot be set when you are not quite sure that you are standing in the same room as your pupils, but tripping over a bush that turns out to be Claire Gray did tend to suggest that things were going quite well. They had been playing camouflage hide-and-seek on the château grounds, and once Jia Liu had been discovered as a rather convincing fence post, the last girl to find was Lily Maguire. She had turned out to be the fountain covered in ivy, and once she had been rescued from her slightly damp hiding place, Good Sister Gwendolyn had introduced the topic of darts. These were not the sort of darts that one threw into a board and counted up the score on, but rather the sort of darts that you threw at your enemies while you were hidden in the shrubbery.

"Let me give you an example of when you might use a dart," said Good Sister Gwendolyn in her most serene manner. "You might be being chased by somebody who wishes you to eat kale and you might not wish to eat kale, and so you might wish to *nicely* dart them with something so that they might have a nap and you may have a bacon sandwich instead." She produced a bag of homemade darts and began to show them to the girls. "All of these have been dipped in the gentlest of sleep potions. Hot chocolate. Milky drinks. Essence of cheese on toast. All of the delightful things that help you sleep. I will demonstrate how to use them and then, if we have time, I will let you try to dart a tree that wishes you ill."

Out of the corner of her eye, she suddenly saw something quite strange. A man had come out of the château carrying a package in his arms. He had stopped and glanced back behind him before—rather peculiarly—walking around the back of the nearest hedge and ducking out of sight. And *anybody* who did this sort of thing was somebody to be studied at some length until it could be decided what they were doing.

Good Sister Gwendolyn turned back to her attentive class, making sure that she could still see the man. "But before all of that, can somebody remind us of what the word *skulking* means? It is relevant, I promise you."

Jia Liu stuck up her hand eagerly. "It is to hide in a dodgy manner and to behave in a dodgy manner and to generally look quite dodgy."

"Excellent," said Good Sister Gwendolyn. "And would we agree that the man coming down the hill toward us is skulking?"

The girls turned around to study him. "Yes," said Katya

Brookes, who had been a most convincing pebble only minutes earlier. "I think so, yes."

"Then I am going to shoot him with a tranquilizing dart," said Good Sister Gwendolyn.

And so she did.

THE PRECISE AIM OF GOOD SISTER GWENDOLYN

Good Sister Gwendolyn's tranquilizer dart hit Raphael on the shoulder. It was a small and yet quite visible dart and the sight of it being in his shoulder made Raphael feel suddenly quite ill. He kept one hand around *Les Roses Blanches*, gently holding the painting against his body and keeping it safe, while he reached up to pull the dart out. For a moment he felt completely fine and then somehow, almost unconsciously, he began to slow down. His run became a walk and then a shuffle. His feet began to feel heavy. His eyes began to close. And for some reason he began to think of his childhood bedroom and his teddy bear collection. He could almost see them in front of him now.

"Fall over," whispered Edie, as the three of them watched him from their hiding place. And then, conscious of the precious thing that he held in his hands, she added: "Carefully."

But it was not to be. Raphael came so close to falling asleep that his legs wobbled and his body began to sink to the ground, but then he stopped. A great gust of cold, sharp air rolled down from the château and straight into his face. His eyes shot open. He shook his head, clearing his thoughts. He took a step forward.

Edie stood up and bellowed, "EXCUSE ME, GOOD SISTER GWENDOLYN, BUT DO YOU HAVE ANY MORE DARTS? BECAUSE IF YOU DO, NOW WOULD BE A GOOD TIME TO USE THEM BECAUSE THIS MAN IS ACTUALLY A THIEF WE ARE TRYING TO CATCH."

Raphael turned around, desperately trying to see where she was.

Good Sister Gwendolyn handed out the darts. Lily Maguire got overexcited and promptly threw hers into her foot. As she sank to the floor with a happy expression on her face, dreaming of chocolate cakes with extra-thick icing, Good Sister Gwendolyn covered her up with a blanket. She turned to the other girls. "Get ready," she said. "Make sure you get him and not anybody else. First rule of darting people: Dart the ones you're meant to dart."

Raphael locked eyes with her. He held the package containing the painting in front of him and gestured at the nearby pond full of dark green water. "If anybody shoots me with anything—and I am looking at you, you weird little children—then I will throw this into the pond."

"That isn't a pond," shrieked Katya Brookes. "That's Sally Campbell! We haven't seen her for hours! Isn't she AMAZING at camouflage?"

Good Sister Gwendolyn glanced at Edie. "What's going on?"

Edie held up her hands. "QUITE A BIT," she said, and then in a calmer voice, "Oh, Good Sister Gwendolyn, as much as I want you to, you cannot dart him. There is a very precious painting in his hands and if he throws it into Sally Campbell, it will be damaged beyond repair, I think. Sorry, Sally, but we cannot risk anything happening to this."

"THAT'S OKAY, BECAUSE I DON'T KNOW WHAT'S GOING ON," said Sally, as she tried to dislodge pond water out of her ears. "THE WATER HAS LEFT ME A BIT DEAF."

"Take the painting," Edie said to Raphael. She held up her hands in defeat. "We shall not follow you."

THE GLORY OF THE INEVITABLE

As Raphael wobbled hastily down the hill, Edie turned to Good Sister Gwendolyn. "Good Sister June has asked for you to join her at the château. She needs you to advise her on various things including sandwiches and also possibly the replenishment of the sock biscuit stash. We shall wait here and innocently make sure this man leaves the garden."

Hanna and Calla made suitably innocent and staying-right-where-they-were expressions.

"I don't believe any of that in the slightest," Good Sister Gwendolyn said with a little smile. "And frankly, I'd be disappointed if you stayed. You know that isn't how we do things in this school. If he's taken something that he shouldn't have, then you get that back from him."

"Then we shall not disappoint you! We shall wait here until it is safe, and then we shall follow him. Subtly! Secretly! Calla has her phone to call for help and Hanna has the knowledge of a thousand books inside her and I know this city like the back of my hand. That man is not getting away from us."

"He won't," replied Good Sister Gwendolyn, as she picked up Lily and started to walk back toward the château. "That cold air might have helped him shake off the worst of that sleeping draft, but it'll still impact his decisions. He won't go far, and he won't be able to think about hiding or doing anything smart. All he'll want to do is stop somewhere safe and have a little nap."

"Perfect," said Edie. "Oh, perfect, perfect, perfect."

EDIE BERGER'S TOP TIPS ON FOLLOWING PERPS[146] WHO HAVE TOLD YOU NOT TO FOLLOW THEM

Just in case you ever find yourself trailing an art thief through the streets of Paris while waiting for the appropriate opportunity to steal back your grandmother's only memory of her first love,[147] I have decided to offer you some advice on what you should do then. And by that, I mean I have asked Edie what she recommends and then I have edited her answers substantially for length because she spent quite some time discussing what we are having for supper,[148] which is interesting but alas, slightly off the point.

1. BE PREPARED AND PRACTICE LOTS. Nobody is good at anything until they practice, and even then nobody will be as good at me at trailing evil-doers across the city I have known all my life. So! You must practice but also reconcile yourself to not

---

146 *Perps* is a way to say "perpetrator" when you are small and French and quite overexcited.

147 It is, I grant, an uncommon scenario, but it could happen to you.

148 Cheese on toast. To be precise, cheese on little chopped-up frankfurters on toast, with ice-cream and sprinkles for dessert.

being the best, but then you will have practiced so much that you are the second best, which is TERRIBLY excellent under the circumstances.

2. BE QUIET. Now, I know you will want to yell for help and attract the attention of people in the street so that they can help you but most people are adults and therefore NOT AS HELPFUL as they could be. Often they will simply tell you not to be so stupid and to stop making noise and "No, that man cannot be stealing something from you for he looks very pleasant and nice," so the best thing is to deal with it yourself and only bring the adults in when you need them.

3. HAVE A NUN DART THEM. Obviously this applies more to those of you who know a nun but if you do and they are good with darts, then you get them to tranquilizer-dart your target because it is So! Useful! For example, the man that we were following walked past the water taxis, barely even looked at the bus stop, and totally ignored the signs for the metro because he was basically sleepwalking at that point and just wanted a nap!

4. BE AWARE. It is EASIER than you think to be followed by people who KNOW you are up to no good, but it is NOT EASY to realize that you are being followed. So! If you are, perhaps, being . followed by a group of purposeful small girls with MONOCLES and MAGNIFYING GLASSES, then you should notice them! And check that they are

following! A handy way is to turn around and walk RIGHT AT THEM and say, "HELLO," because if they are British, then they will faint at being talked to by a stranger and *VOILÀ*, they cannot tail you ANY LONGER.

5. BE READY TO ADMIT:
   a. when you have been spotted, and
   b. when the person you are following is actually leading you in a massive circle . . .

THE UNEXPECTED CIRCLES OF RAPHAEL GAGNON

"Isn't it strange, though, how we keep going down the same streets?" said Calla. "We have gone past this bread shop a lot and also we have gone past this restaurant and ACTUALLY I think we have also gone past this bus stop a lot as well."

Hanna looked blank. "But why is he doing that? I'm doing all of my best tradecraft. I'm blending into the street as we speak! He can't have spotted us. Maybe he's lost."

"He is not lost," said Edie, who had, of course, worked this out a long time ago. She had just not wished to admit it to either her friends or herself. "I think that even though he is very tired and suffering the effects of the dart, he still knows that he's being followed."

A little voice inside her head whispered: *And he knows who's following him.*

They watched the man walk to the edge of the river and lean against a wall in a manner that any tourist would have thought impeccably Parisian but that any Parisian would have found impeccably suspicious. As a result, many of the local people had given him a wide berth,[149] and all that stood

---

149 This is quite a strange expression but it basically means "not going very

between him and Edie, Calla, and Hanna was a crowd of tourists waiting for one of the guided river tours.

Edie pulled her friends back, so that they were standing under the shade of a shop. In the distance she saw the corner that marked the beginning of the Rue de la Vérité and a little part of her heart lifted at the sight. She understood Paris. She knew this city. She had been brought up with it. And even though the man had spotted them following him, it was not over yet.

"I feel a little bit sick," Calla said faintly. "And honestly, I'm not sure whether it's nerves or the fact that I've not eaten for a whole hour."

Edie squeezed her arm. "It is nerves," she said. "I used to have them, but I do not anymore. It is a question of willpower. Do not be scared. And if you are scared, you must just remember it is because you care about something very much. There is nothing in this world to ever be afraid of. There is so much more to care about. For example, I care about baklava very much."

In the distance, she watched the tourist boat pull up. The thief saw it too and stepped back to allow the tourists to get on and off. There were so many of them that he had to move completely to the side. The only problem was that he caught sight of the three girls following him. For a moment they stared at each other in shock until he slowly began to shake his head. This was partially due to the fact that he wanted the

....

close to scary and weird things that you do not want to be close to," and here is a sentence in which you could use it: "I am giving a wide berth to that broccoli cupcake."

240

peace and quiet of his bedroom, but also because Edie was glaring at him in a very ferocious fashion. "I have your painting," he said eventually. "And also, I am fairly sure that I told you not to follow me."

"Coincidence!" Hanna said brightly. "We are on holiday in Paris and just *happened* to come across you. How nice it is to see somebody that we know. Perhaps we can go and have some cake together and pretend that none of this ever happened."

"Not an option," said Raphael as he stifled a long and heartfelt yawn. "My client would not approve of it in the slightest." He glanced at the river and then back at the girls. "Look, I am going to give you one last chance to stop whatever it is that you're doing. I don't want this to end poorly, but it is your choice. And it will not go well if you keep following me."

"It's a *coincidence*," said Hanna.

"It is not," said Edie. "Give me back that painting."

"No," said Raphael. "Look at the river. Do you see it? I am fairly sure that this time it is an actual river and not, you know, one of your friends. What sort of a school allows such things? I do not understand it. But I'll tell you what I do understand, and that is this." He held the package out and above the water. "You do not want me to drop this painting."

"You wouldn't—" said Hanna.

"I think he might," said Calla.

"I am going to make you regret the day you ever met me," said Edie.

The man smiled. He pulled the painting back to safety. "Go," he said. "Talk to your friends. Decide what you wish to do. I will wait here for an answer. Make your choice wisely. Think of the painting."

FOR A MOMENT, ALL WAS LOST

"What do we do?" Hanna said softly. "This wasn't mentioned in *any* of my guidebooks."

Edie thought very quickly. "We have to buy time, and right now I do not think that we have much choice. We have to do what he says. He is going to throw the painting in the river if we keep following him. And this time the river is an actual river and not just the excellently camouflaged Sally Campbell. I do not think that we can do anything but back away. Properly, this time."

"He wouldn't throw it into the river," said Calla, looking at the man and then back at Edie and Hanna. "Would he? I mean, he's been trying to steal it forever and now he's going to throw it away? It's not particularly the most straightforward thing to do."

"We cannot risk making it happen," said Edie. "Once upon a time I met a man in a café who insisted that shakshuka[150]

----

150 Shakshuka is eggs in tomato and garlic and rice, and you have not lived until you have tried Marianne's version of it. Obviously you have lived, because you are reading this, so I am speaking *metaphorically* and not

was best served without coriander and my dear maman practically fainted over the horrors of it all. We had to stop her from marching into the kitchen and telling him the error of his ways. Anyway! We are not here to talk about eggs, delicious and as wonderful as they are; we are here to stop the last memory that my grand-mère has of her first love from ending up in the river and that, I think, means that we must be devious. We must allow him to think we are doing precisely what he wants us to do, when in fact, we are playing for time."

"How do you actually play for time, though?" said Calla. "Because that just sounds confusing."

"It is a metaphor, my delightfully literal fruit loop," said Edie. "Now put your hands up."

Calla took a deep and very British breath. "That's going to make *everyone* look at us."

"I have spent my life being looked at," said Edie. She stepped forward and lifted up her arms dramatically, pirouetting as she did so that she had her back to the man and her eyes on Calla. "We are *twelve years old*," she said. "Adults are *trained* to ignore us. And so we must use that to our advantage. All they will see is three girls, and nobody knows what to do with three young girls, so they will not look at us a moment longer than they have to. But *he* will understand what we mean by it, and know that we are giving up, and then he will not drop the painting into the Seine. And that, my friends, is a satisfactory outcome for all concerned."

....

actually. Obviously if you are actually dead and reading this, that is a whole different situation altogether.

Calla and Hanna slowly held up their hands.

Edie turned so she could watch Raphael. A slow smile slid across her face as she realized that it was working. He was buying it. "He thinks he has won. Well done, my friends."

"But he has won," said Calla. "We've literally all got our hands up."

"I think she's got a point," said Hanna.

"He has won the battle but not the war," said Edie. "For at last, our reinforcements have arrived."

THERE IS NOTHING BETTER THAN A PLAN COMING TOGETHER

Just before they had left the château, Edie had asked Good Sister June to make two phone calls.

And this is the moment where I tell you precisely what Edie had said.

"We are not going to be able to save the painting ourselves. I would like to, but I am practical and know that we cannot. Paris is big and that horrible man could go anywhere. Plus he *knows* us now so once he sees us, we'll have to stop and let him get away. But he does not know the others and so they shall take over when we have to let him go. They will trail him throughout the streets of the city and then, when he stops, we shall strike."

She had paused here in a Dramatic Fashion[151] before continuing.

"Good Sister June, please, I need you to get some of the other girls to meet us. They can track where we are using Calla's phone. Hanna and I set up an app on it so we can always find her.[152] If they use it, they will find us wherever we are.

---

151 For she is, after all, only human.

152 Calla, faintly: "Why did I not know about this?"
    Hanna, supportively: "We didn't want to misplace you. Like socks. You know."

But! They must not admit that they know us. They must just be walking on the street and then begin to tail the man the moment he thinks he is getting rid of us. So please will you talk to the others and send me the girls that are especially good in a crisis, the girls who are talented at trailing perpetrators of foul deeds, and all the ones who can make an excellent sandwich because I am *ravenous*."

And so Good Sister June had done precisely what she had been told to do, with the result that Eloise and Claire Taylor, Lucy Millais, Sethi and Sabia Gopal, Maisie Holloway, and Rose Bastable, with the added bonus of Good Sister Christine, were all now on the Parisian streets and taking great pains to pretend to not recognize each other. Good Sister Christine, who had managed to find a raincoat from somewhere and a remarkably convincing Germanic accent, was enjoying herself by asking for directions. Lucy and Maisie had paired off to take selfies against the backdrop of the river, whilst Sethi and Sabia had found a bench on which to do impromptu aerobics. Eloise and Claire had gone into the nearest boulangerie and purchased several particularly tempting baguettes, which Rose Bastable was in the process of turning into sandwiches on a camp table that she had produced with a flourish out of her backpack.[153]

"Oh, they are *good*," whispered Edie. A part of her knew that she was very close to giving the game away and so she distracted herself by faking a sudden and quite intent interest in Calla's socks. Calla, who was not aware of this, made a *What are you doing?* face and poked Edie in the stomach.

....

153 Small table. Big backpack.

Hanna said, "He's leaving."

Sethi and Sabia Gopal stretched and began to nonchalantly walk down the street after him. Good Sister Christine suddenly realized that the place she'd been looking for was in that very same direction. Lucy Millais and Maisie Holloway shifted, ever so slightly, and began to take selfies with the thief in the background of them, and Eloise and Claire Taylor began to meander down the street after him.

"There's nothing that man will do now without us knowing *all* about it," said Rose, coming over to talk to Calla, Hanna, and Edie. "The only thing we didn't know was the base of operations—where we report back to and plan the next step. Good Sister Gwendolyn says that you should *always* have a base of operations."

"We are using my mother's plant shop on the Rue de la Vérité," said Edie, as if she had not just figured this out seconds earlier. "Isabelle is going to let us in. Not only is it useful because of how much space it offers for us to utilize purposefully and effectively, but all the buildings on that street—and indeed, all around it—are connected by their roofs and attics. If he stops nearby—and he will, because of Good Sister Gwendolyn's dart—then we'll find the building and, perhaps, be able to get in through the roof."

"What if he's got a car or something waiting to pick him up? There might be an accomplice," said Hanna, who had read a substantial amount of Agatha Christie. "There *always* has to be an accomplice."

Edie gave her a wise and comforting smile. "There might be an accomplice, but nobody drives in Paris. Seriously, you do not get *anywhere* in an emergency. Once, we lost my mother for three weeks in a traffic jam and all she had done was to drive to the boulangerie in the next arrondissement."

Calla decided to firmly change the subject. "We need to think about what we do if he does have an accomplice. We have to be practical." She paused and then, suddenly excited, said, "We could actually get some of the first-years involved and use them to watch the roads. We'll be able to get a message to them if he gets away from us. We'll be able to tell the police where he's gone and what to look for. Is that possible, Edie? Or are there too many roads to keep an eye on?"

"They can watch the closest exits on the Périph,"[154] said Edie. "If he's in a car and trying to get away, then that's where he'll go. Text the first-years and tell them to head for the busy, big road that we drove in on when we arrived. If they follow the traffic they will find it. Tell them to go carefully! I do not want squished first-years on my conscience."

"And if he doesn't get in a car, we'll track him ourselves," Hanna said in a deeply practical manner.

"Perfect," said Calla. She began to fire off texts on her phone.

"Clearly, it would be *much* more considerate if he stays on foot," Edie said in a thoughtful fashion. "I have read that most stolen goods do not actually travel far and are often closer than you think.[155] Anyway! We shall go to the plant shop and cross our fingers that he stays local, for if he does, it is *perfectly*

---

154 This is a fancy word for the *Périphérique*, which is a fancy word for a road that goes around the middle of Paris in a great circle and connects everywhere to everywhere else.

155 She had read this in *Pilfering for Beginners*, which is a very detailed book.

doable to hop from one building to another. For example, when I was younger,[156] I once made my way to school on the rooftops alone—"

"Just like in *Rooftoppers*," said Hanna with a dreamy look in her eyes. "Oh, how *perfect*."

"Isabelle had to hide me in the shop for a week to let my grand-mère get over it all," said Edie in an equally dreamy manner.

"If either of you want to focus for a minute," said Calla, waving her phone in their faces, "I just got a text from Sethi. She says that he's gone to ground on the Rue de la République. Apparently, he was walking so slowly that he was practically sleepwalking. They've got him surrounded and Good Sister Christine is even having her dinner at the café two doors down from where he is.[157] The moment he moves, one of them will spot it."

"Perfect," said Edie, "because we are about to end this chapter and move on to the next part of the plan."[158]

....

156 I appreciate that this sounds very elderly, but then I suppose that being twelve and thinking about the things that you did when you were four can make you feel like that.

157 She had left her raincoat behind on a bench along with her German accent, and was now pretending to be a famous chef from London who had been sent to try every dish in Paris. At least twice.

158 Obviously she did not say that, but I am sure she *meant* it.

IN WHICH WE RETURN TO THE RUE DE LA VÉRITÉ

When she had been sent away from Paris, Edie had taken it with her inside her heart. All of her memories of her wild and beautiful childhood, and all of the stories that her parents had told her, and all of the protests that she'd been on, all of it nestled deep inside of her. Her parents. Her family. The three of them standing together on the street, marching with a thousand other voices at her back. It had been why she had not been able to settle in England, even when Good Sister June had made her cheese on toast and the two of them had discussed at length the qualities of a perfect macaron. A little part of her had been still in Paris and unable to let it go.

But as she led Hanna and Calla along the Rue de la Vérité, she began to realize how much she had forgotten.

She had forgotten the way that each shop on the street had a separate color, and how when the light hit them they could look like a row of macarons nestled together in a box and wrapped in snow-white tissue paper. She had forgotten the way that, just above the shops, there were people living in flats and apartments and how sometimes, when their windows were open and the wind was just right, you could hear what they were watching on the television or singing in the shower. And most of all, she had forgotten the way that her mother's plant shop sat at the heart of it all, glowing like a dark green jewel in the late-afternoon sun.

At her side, Calla let out a little sigh of joy. "It's like a real-life postcard."

Hanna suddenly turned to Edie. Her eyes were bright and a little bit feverish. "Did a man called Ludwig Bemelmans ever live here? Or a small boy named Pepito who was the son of the Spanish ambassador?"

"Everything is possible in Paris," said Edie, who hadn't understood any of this remarkable speech at all. She decided to distract them by pointing out a very familiar chocolate shop,[159] an equally familiar brasserie,[160] and the bench that was dedicated to Monsieur Abadie, before they arrived outside of the plant shop. It was almost covered in roses, pinks and scarlets and reds, all tumbling together to blanket the walls in color, while the front window was full of terra-cotta plant pots. Tiny, spiky succulents sat next to enormous ferns; in one corner, an Egyptian walking onion had spent the last few years gently meandering across the floor, whilst in another,

....

159 Where Madame Laurentis had caught sight of the three girls—or rather, had caught sight of Edie's remarkable hair peering over the top of the piled-up sweets in the shop window—and promptly dropped a box of toffee from both shock and delight. Luckily enough, it was a small box, and she managed to keep it off the floor with some remarkable keepy-up skills.

160 Where Frau Bettelstein and Herr Bettelstein turned to each other in the middle of their afternoon tea service and said, "Oh, did you see her? I think she's back—she's back! At last!"

something that was covered with red berries lay across an entire shelf.

And in the middle of all of this was a woman who looked as if she'd seen a ghost.

"Edie?" she said. "Is it you? Are you back?"

THE WOMAN WHO THOUGHT SHE'D SEEN A GHOST

"It IS me," said Edie in her most reassuring tone of voice. "Dear Isabelle, I am BACK, and yes, okay, I shall permit you to hug me just a tiny bit but just so you do not do anything inconveniently dramatic, for we do not have much time."

Isabelle was a tall and solid woman, the sort who was never shocked or surprised for long, and so she grinned with happiness as she wrapped her arms around Edie and hugged her tight. "My dear one, it has been *years* since I saw you, and you tell me not to hug you? Especially after I know you've been in town for two days and not been to see me or the shop until now?"

"I have been very busy! And I will catch you up the moment that I can on it, but for now we do not have the time. We are *sort of* in the middle of a small and emphatic crisis! We need to use the shop and maybe use it overnight and possibly also solve a crime with the help of everything inside it, and is all that all right with you?"

Isabelle let Edie go. "Of course it is. I trust you entirely; you know that."[161]

....

161 And when she said this, Edie permitted Isabelle to give her a little bit of a longer hug.

"Excellent," said Edie. "Also! We will be making a package that will look like a painting and be enough to fool the thief,[162] but! In case there is not enough *stuff* down there, we may need to ask you to bring us some more supplies. And if we do, perhaps you could also bring us some fresh bread and some cheese and some charcuterie to snack on, for my stomach is rapidly diminishing. Thank you!"

---

162 Hanna to Isabelle, sympathetically: "It will make sense soon, I promise."

PLOTTING IN THE PLANT SHOP

The plant shop had seen many revolutions in its life, and the memory of these were written on the walls. It had sun-bleached posters stuck up between the trailing plants and painted slogans written in faded paint on the walls behind the compost. One poster had a picture of a woman in a blue shirt, wearing a red headscarf, with her sleeve rolled up to show a muscle and a small, satisfied smile on her face. Next to her, somebody had painted a long slogan on the wall: *Nous sommes toutes des héroïnes*[163] and next to that, somebody had scrawled in English: *I do not wish women to have power over men; but over themselves,*[164] and just above those: *It is never too late to be what you might have been.*[165]

163 This means in English: "We are all heroines," and it is a very good sentiment indeed.

164 This is a quote by a remarkable lady called Mary Wollstonecraft and she was a very good egg indeed. I think, because of that, her favorite cake would have been a Victoria sponge.

165 This is a quote by a remarkable lady called George Eliot. She was apparently very fond of marmalade cake and went so far as to invent her own recipe for it. Good Sister Honey is in the process of perfecting it as we speak. I am helping her out by Nobly Eating the Failed Attempts.

"I feel like I want to take over the world," Calla said as she studied it all, wide-eyed. "And if you actually really did grow up here, then I get why you are the way you are."

"Where else could I have grown up but here?" Edie said happily. Even though Isabelle had rearranged things and tidied up, the shop had not changed one bit. It felt like Marianne might walk out of the back room at any moment, or that Jean-Claude might come in through the front door with his shopping. For a moment she had to let it all soak in. It was the nearest she'd been to her parents in years. She could almost *hear* them.

It was a little bit like having her heart made whole.

A loud noise in the corner made her rapidly come back down to earth. She turned around to see Hanna pulling empty boxes and pieces of cardboard out from a cupboard. "Oh, Hanna, my sweet little savory pumpkin head. What on earth are you doing? Isabelle has *entrusted* us with not demolishing the shop[166] and here you are doing that very thing the precise moment that she leaves."

"I'm making those packages look like the fake painting," said Hanna. "If we're going to trick him with them, they need to look right. Did you see the paper that he'd wrapped it up in? It has to look exactly the same or else he'll see us coming a mile off. He can't question it." She studied the cardboard carefully. "This will work, providing he's still a bit sleepy and distracted. The problem will come when he's not."

"Then we will have another distraction ready for him,"

---

[166] Isabelle, handing the keys over: "Please do not demolish the shop."

replied Edie in her most calming manner. She headed over to where her mother used to keep the brown paper to wrap the plants in, and everything was just as Marianne had left it. The paper was piled up next to several faded leaflets about protests and demonstrations that had happened many years ago. One of them even had Marianne's writing still on it. Edie put this one gently into her pocket before giving the rest of the paper to Hanna. "Do you need anything else?"

Hanna shook her head. "I think it will work," she said. She studied the boxes with satisfaction. "But you're going to have to figure out how we break in to get the painting back. We can't just use the front door. We need to surprise him. He's already threatened the painting twice. We can't run the risk of him doing anything to it." She paused for a moment. "Honestly, I don't know why I'm telling you this stuff, because I know you'll have thought about it already."

"You are telling me because that is the sort of person you are and the sort of person *I* am," Edie said with satisfaction. She poked Calla in the side. "Will you text Rose and get her to come over here? Like, yesterday? I am going to need her."

IT'S HARD WORK BEING A THIEF

We must leave the girls there for a brief moment while we go to join Raphael Gagnon in a small building on the Rue de la République. It was a very normal-looking building with a front door that helped it look like any other. The only difference was this door had a built-in facial recognition system and a fingerprint scanner that only recognized Raphael.[167] Once inside, you walked into a building that was only one room wide and almost completely bare except for a sofa, a fridge, a television, and a very small table.[168] Raphael kept the fridge packed full of cheese and sausage and a carton of long-life milk so that whenever he needed to, he could have a quick meal. He also kept an emergency blanket and pillow tucked underneath the sofa so if he needed somewhere to spend the night, he could. He really was a very practical thief.

....

167 Except it did not recognize him with a fake beard on. He had discovered this during a Previous Exploit and had had to quickly take off his beard in the street. It really was quite the close shave.

168 There was of course a tiny bathroom tucked away for emergencies of that nature, but I'm about to go to lunch and really don't want to give any more details than I have to.

The moment that he'd gotten inside that building with *Les Roses Blanches*, he'd laid the canvas gently on a cushion on the table before moving it to the center of the room and underneath the skylight. This was a big window in the roof that he had used to escape through several times in the past and so, along with keeping it free of cumbersome security systems,[169] he also used it as a spotlight so that he could keep an eye on whatever he had stolen, wherever he was in the building.

It was only when he'd done all of this that he sat down to relax and the magic of Good Sister Gwendolyn's tranquilizer dart began to properly work. It started with a long and heartfelt yawn as he snuggled down into the sofa. He reached for the blanket and began to wrap himself up in it. His eyes slowly closed. For some reason, he began to think of hot chocolate.

And so it was because of all of this that he did not notice the small girl being lowered from the roof above him.

---

169 For there is nothing worse than needing to make a quick exit but not remembering the password to open the door. Trust me on this, for reasons that I cannot remotely elaborate upon here.

A FLASHBACK OF FREESIAS

The dangling girl's name was Edie Berger[170] and she was in the process of stealing the painting back.

And this is how it happened.

After Rose had arrived in the plant shop as requested, and the four of them had eaten their emergency sock biscuits, they had split up. Hanna and Calla had carried all of the fake painting packages from the plant shop over to Raphael's building before distributing them carefully among the girls. Several passing tourists looked quite interested but were rapidly distracted when Lucy Millais and Maisie Holloway began to talk to them about chocolate ganache and fish finger sandwiches. Hanna and Calla stayed at the side of the street until they were sure that the coast was clear before ushering everybody up the fire escape with their packages. Eloise Taylor had to go back and get her package on three separate occasions

---

170 They had considered using Eloise Taylor, who had shown a particular talent for dangling from things. She had not yet, however, shown a talent for actually doing things whilst being dangled.

but eventually all the girls, save those who were watching the door, were on the top of the building.

Whilst this was happening, Rose and Edie had been in the plant shop. They had been looking for the biggest and strongest plant that they could find and eventually settled on a plant named Suzette.[171] Suzette was an enormous vine who had been alive for longer than Edie herself and during that time had grown to roughly twice the height and width of the front window. Instead of stalks or petals, she had enormous lianas, which is a fancy word for a very long and very firm bit of plant that looks and acts very much like rope.

Rose apologized politely to Suzette whilst Edie began to cut one of the vines away from the main body of the plant. It took Edie quite a while because the vine was as thick as her arm, but eventually she made it work and the two of them raced off to the Rue de la République with a very heavy plant on their shoulders.[172]

Getting it to the top of the building, however, was another

....

171 Marianne had named Suzette after one of her favorite desserts in the entire world: Crêpes Suzette. Crêpes are a type of very thin and especially delicious pancake, but Pancake does not necessarily make an excellent name for a plant.

172 Bearing in mind that they were doing most of this during the late afternoon, the girls were seen by a substantial number of people and, inevitably, these people had questions about why they were carrying a large plant through the streets. Edie has told me that this is what she said: *"Il n'y a pas de quoi s'inquiéter. Dites-moi plutôt votre biscuit préféré."* Which, roughly translated, means: "There is nothing to worry about. Tell me instead about your favorite biscuit," which is really the sort of very useful French that everybody should learn.

issue entirely. Suzette was so long and bulky that they needed the help of a small army of first-years to pull it up the fire escape, and then they had to post several further small children on either side of the roof as they knotted it around the pointy bits of the building in a safe and secure fashion. Several of the first-years were also made to sit on one end of the vine to weigh Suzette down and keep her in place whilst the others seized the opportunity to eat their emergency sock biscuits.

"Are you all paying attention?" said Hanna, deciding to make use of the fact that everybody was suddenly very silent and attentive. "Good. So anybody who doesn't have a package already needs to make sure that they pick one up, and you all need to remember the plan. These are fake packages and that man needs to think that they're the real thing. All *you* have to do is head for the Rue de la Vérité and then the château. If he gets near you, drop your package and don't look back. You don't have to be scared of him, but there's no point in risking anything." She turned back to Edie. "Are you ready?"

Edie nodded as Lucy Millais and Maisie Holloway began to carefully wrap one end of Suzette around her waist. Once they were finished, they knotted the ends together and secured them with a mix of rapidly donated scrunchies, hair clips, and a remarkable number of odd socks. When they were done, Edie gave the knots a quick tug with her free hand. "Excellent work! Now, gather around me!"

"Not you," said Calla warningly to the four girls who were sitting on the end of Suzette. "You stay exactly where you are. You can listen from there."

Edie gave her a Look. "Calla! Stop talking! Pay attention! It is time for my inspiring speech! We might die tonight! Admittedly we might die at any point, so it is better to die a glorious death on the rooftops of Paris, no? Where is more beautiful than this? So! Potential death! But also, we shall WIN! And! I shall console anybody of a nervous disposition by telling them that if they do die in this GLORIOUS endeavor, then we shall find an artist to immortalize them in a painting that we shall then place within a museum devoted solely to their great deeds! A treat!"

"Now come on, everybody," said Hanna. "It's time to dangle my best friend off the roof."

THE DANGLING OF EDIE BERGER

I would like you to imagine something very tightly wrapped around your middle. Perhaps it is a belt that you've pulled a little bit too tight, or the grip of a small and quite persistent younger sibling who does not wish to let go of you. Either way, this thing is very tight and growing tighter all the time. In fact, it has grown so tight that there is a part of you that thinks it might actually go all the way through you and chop your legs off and leave you in two separate pieces on the floor.[173]

This was precisely how Edie felt as the others lowered her down. She tried to ignore the feeling of being sliced in two and instead focus on the task at hand. The painting was just below her and the thief had his eyes closed. His whole body was relaxed. A part of her could almost hear him snoring. It was the perfect time to swap the painting with the package she held in her hands. They were practically identical. Hanna had done an amazing job.

....

173 I know this is very dramatic, but Edie has dictated this section word for word, and as I have not dangled off a building and she has, I am inclined to let her have it.

The only problem was the fact that Lucy Millais and Maisie Holloway, who were the people in charge of lowering Suzette the liana, were developing very sweaty hands. It was not the sort of thing that they could confess easily, for they did not have the spare breath with which to do so,[174] and so both of them thought positive thoughts and hoped very hard for the best. The best, however, turned into the liana suddenly skidding through their hands and Edie plummeting toward the painting with alarming speed. She was only stopped when Calla, Hanna, and several first-years who had startlingly quick reflexes grabbed the rapidly disappearing liana and pulled it back under control.

Hanna peered in through the top window and made a cheery thumbs-up gesture at Edie.

Who, despite being upside down, and feeling very much like the filling in the middle of a custard cream, managed to make a *Yes Everything Is Okay and I Am Fine Thanks for Asking but We Should Definitely Get On with This* face in response.

Hanna made a *Well You Don't Have to Look Like That I'm Only Trying to Help Oh Isn't It Useful That He's Asleep We Should Get On with Things* face back at her.

Edie made a *Yes That is Entirely My Point* face before she started to descend again. This time it was steady and controlled and not the sort of descent that made her do impromptu somersaults and almost drop the fake package on top of the thief's head. For a moment she wondered if he might have woken up, but he looked even more asleep than he had before.

....

174 It turns out that lowering a petite yet quite sturdy twelve-year-old takes a fair bit of effort.

Up on the roof, Hanna whispered, "Just a little bit more" to the others still holding the liana.

Lucy and Maisie took deep breaths.

Calla sent a *Not Now Mum I'm a Bit Busy* text with her free hand.

Rose Bastable began to make jam sandwiches for several quite hungry first-years.

Edie's fingers touched the top of the painting.

And Raphael Gagnon opened his eyes.

MISSION NOT-QUITE-PROBABLE

It was then that several things happened in quick succession, and because they all happened one after the other, I shall put them into a numbered list for you.[175]

1. Hanna yelled, "TAKE HER DOWN," and Edie swooped toward the painting and wrapped her arms around it. The moment this happened, Hanna yelled, "TAKE HER UP!"
2. Several of the first-years were distracted by the smell of freshly cooked fish fingers on the wind and thus, let go of the liana.
3. With the inevitable result that Edie flew back down toward the waiting figure of Raphael.
4. Hanna said something very rude[176] before throwing

---

175 You might think that this is because I have mastered the art of the bullet point and have now moved onto advanced formatting and am thus seeking any opportunity to demonstrate my skills, and you would be quite right.

176 "KALE CUPCAKES!"

herself and also several of the nearest first-years back onto the rapidly disappearing liana.

5. Edie completed a rather remarkable somersault as she was pulled in a forthright fashion back up to the ceiling.

6. Her shoe fell off and clonked[177] Raphael on the head.[178]

7. And Raphael fell unconscious to the floor.

---

177 I have queried the word *clonked* with Edie and Calla and they have both assured me that is the right word for the moment. "You have to say it out loud to get the full impact," said Calla when I spoke to her. "That's exactly what it sounded like."

178 He really was having a very bad day indeed.

THE NINE POISONS OF HANNA KOWALCZYK

There is not much that one can do under such circumstances other than run, and so the girls did. Once they had hoisted Edie back up onto the roof and disentangled her from Suzette, the girls disappeared. Several of them headed down the fire escape at the front of the building, whilst others lowered the rest of Suzette down the back of the building and began to carefully climb down her. Some of the taller girls jumped from Raphael's building and onto the one next door before swinging down a series of balconies and Usefully Open Windows.

As she watched them leave, Edie kicked off her remaining shoe so that she could go barefoot. She checked that her insides were still together and that the vine had not cut her in two, and then turned to Calla. "Calla, my wonderful little jam tart, please may I borrow your phone? When that man awakes, he will be most upset, so I think it might be useful if we have something else to distract him with, and being suspended upside down has helped me figure out precisely what that thing needs to be."

"I know nine types of poison,"[179] Hanna said in a rather remarkable manner as Calla handed over her phone. "I can use them if we need to."

"There is no need for poison! You have me, and I have Paris. There is a whole city full of people to help us in our Noble Quest, and I am about to tell them what we need. And also, if I have time, I will order us dinner for when we are done. There is a wonderful restaurant that will deliver to the château, and I am going to be very hungry when all of this is done."

Calla glanced back at Hanna. "Will all our school trips be like this?"

"Yes," Hanna said happily. "Isn't it great?"

---

179 1. Cold Kale Soup. 2. Toothpaste and Orange Juice. 3. Spinach. 4. Slightly Too-Squishy Broccoli. 5. Pureed Parsnip. 6. Raisins. 7. Beetroot. 8. Spoiled Milk. 9. The Skin off Rice Pudding.

EDIE'S DISTRACTION

When Edie had finished her last call, she turned to Hanna and Calla. "Okay," she said, handing the phone back. "The first thing we need to do is to get off the roof. Within seconds he is going to come awake and he is going to try to figure out where I am. I have to be somewhere other than here; otherwise all of this will have been for nothing."

"Then enough talking," replied Hanna.

The three of them ran down the fire escape in record time and arrived at street level just to see Raphael stumble out of the house. He shook his head two or three times as though he was trying to remember where he was and had to reach out to the wall to stop himself from falling over. The bruise on his forehead in the shape of Edie's shoe was rapidly turning black and blue.

It was only when he caught sight of a group of first-years, standing by the fountain at the far end of the street, that Raphael seemed to remember what was happening. With a roar, he leapt forward and cornered Eloise Taylor almost instantly.[180] She flung her fake package at him and slid out

---

180 Eloise is terribly good at dangling off things, but she is not very good at running away when she is meant to.

of his grasp before racing away down the street. He let her go and concentrated his attention on the package. He tore it open and flung the paper on the ground. And when he realized that it contained nothing but air and empty seed packets, he said something incredibly rude.[181]

Edie jerked her thumb toward the end of the road. "Go ahead," she said to Hanna and Calla. "I will catch up with you. There is something that I must do first." She pushed the two of them in the direction that she had indicated and then, only when she was sure that they were safely away and lost in the crowds, did she turn to face Raphael. Their eyes met. He slowed to a walk. Edie held up her own painting-shaped package. She pulled what she hoped was a suitably *I'm Just an Innocent Girl Please Don't Be Mean* expression. A small smile slid across Raphael's face[182] and he nodded. He made a *You're Quite Irritating but Just Give Me Back the Painting and We'll Forget This Ever Happened* expression.

She waited until he was within arm's reach of her before taking a step back.

And bellowing a very long and very loud sentence in French.[183]

....

181 "BUTTERED PARSNIPS!"
182 Just underneath a rapidly forming bruise in the shape of the sole of Edie's shoe.
183 I do not know how else to describe the sound that she made other than it was remarkably evocative of an elephant who has stood on some Legos.

TWELVE WORDS

"Cet homme croit que le fromage anglais est meilleur que le français."

Which in English means: "This man believes English cheese is better than French."

And, in Paris, it caused chaos.

A *FROMAGE* FRACAS

Raphael first realized that something was wrong when somebody from three floors up tipped a bowl of soapy dishwashing liquid onto his head. He realized that something was definitely wrong when an old lady standing next to him poked him in the arm with her parasol and another came over to stamp firmly on his foot. Somebody who was carefully putting out their laundry on the balcony began to throw socks at him, while a local shop owner began to very deliberately pelt him with small fragments of Camembert.

In short, he was being noticed, and this was something that no thief wishes to be.

And all the while, Hanna and Edie and Calla were getting farther away from him.

The three girls skidded out of the Rue de la République and began to head in the direction of the Rue de la Vérité. The sun had almost completely set now, and the shadows on the street were long and dark and Edie was enjoying the moment more than she rather thought she should. She began to jog backward to try to explain it to her friends. "I *know* that we are in a life-or-death situation but I am enjoying this moment rather more than I think I should. Consider how great and noble this is. We are reuniting my dear grand-mère with the only memory of her long-lost love, and we are doing so in Paris, the most romantic and most beautiful and generally most best city on earth!"

"But that man will know exactly where we're going," said Calla, who was focused on the matter at hand. "He's going to find us there. He knows it's the quickest way back to the château." She glanced nervously behind them. It was as if she almost expected him to appear at that precise moment.

"Of course he knows where we're going," said Edie. She looked at the others with a satisfied smile. "In fact, I am rather counting on it."

THE RISING OF THE RUE DE LA VÉRITÉ

Raphael did indeed know where they were going. The moment that he'd disentangled himself from the Roquefort-wielding rioters of Paris, he'd dodged back inside his house and out of a secret back door. Several quick bouts of lock-picking and wall-climbing later, he was standing in an alleyway opposite the Rue de la Vérité.

As he stood there and tried to get his scattered thoughts and exhausted body together, he saw one of the girls—the one who had thrown her shoe at him and briefly knocked him out—standing opposite him. Precisely where he'd thought she would be. She wasn't with the other girls anymore, but that didn't matter. She still held the painting in her arms. That was the important thing.

A little feeling of satisfaction began to form inside his stomach. The painting was practically his. He knew that there was only one way out of that street and that was back up to the château. If the girls were going to take the picture to the house, then he would simply steal it back. He knew every inch of that building by now and how to deal with it. If the police were there, then he'd just wait until they weren't. The garden was big enough to hide in without being discovered.[184] All he had to do was stay calm. And in control. And also awake.

He took a slow and squelchy step forward. The dishwashing water that Madame Fournier of the third floor had thrown on him had gone all the way through to his socks. The sensation was particularly unpleasant. His foot kept slipping around in his shoe and he had the vague idea that he might have some of her leftover dinner stuck in his hair.

As he got closer, the girl on the corner looked up. Raphael froze very precisely where he was and tried to imagine himself invisible. He was not sure that it helped, but it did create a reaction because the girl opposite him suddenly raced around the corner and disappeared. For a moment, his sleepy mind wondered if he had actually turned invisible. It was quite possible. A lot of unexpected things were happening.

But then she reappeared and looked right at him.

"Hello," she said. "You do not have to hide, you know. I do see you over there."

Raphael stepped out. "I'm here for the painting," he said.

The girl sighed. "When will you realize that you *cannot* have it? The painting belongs to my family. We will never let it go. And I will not give it to you now, or ever. You need to understand that and GO HOME."

"You don't deserve it," said Raphael. "I'm not going anywhere." He wiped some dishwater out of his eyes and began to walk forward down the street, toward the small and annoying child. If he had been more awake, I think he might have

---

184 As Odette knew very well.

noticed how she was leading him down the road in a very particular manner, but he did not. All he noticed was how she was starting to look satisfactorily worried, and how close the painting was.

"We don't have to do this," said Raphael, matching her step for step. "Give me the painting. It's just you and me now. I don't see your friends anymore."

It was then that she did the most curious thing.

She smiled.

THE TRUFFLES OF WAR

"Let loose the truffles of war!" said Edie, for of course it was her and this was all quite deliberately part of her plan.

The windows nearest Raphael opened to reveal an army of first-years, armed with freshly made chocolate truffles. These had been donated to the cause by Madame Laurentis, who now stood in the center window like an avenging angel. She gave the command to fire and the sky grew dark with truffles as the girls launched them at Raphael. Jia Liu managed to get her truffle to hit his left ear, while Ellen Beaufort achieved the remarkable aim of shooting several truffles up his nose. Under this assault, Raphael had no option but to fall to his knees and say something very rude.[185]

"SPECTACULAR," shrieked Edie, who was almost paralytic with excitement.

With a roar, Raphael stumbled forward.

The only problem was that this was when Herr and Frau Bettelstein began their part of the attack. Edie had been quite specific as to her requirements on her telephone call to them

....

185 "COLD RICE PUDDING WITH A SKIN ON TOP!"

earlier and they had been very happy to deliver. Herr Bettelstein had closed the brasserie early while his wife had collected up all of their leftover black rye bread. It had dried out so much that it was solid and hard; a perfect missile to be thrown at the bad man who was chasing Edie and her friends. Frau Bettelstein, a champion netball player in her youth, was particularly talented at this endeavor and managed to fling a very hard lump of bread right in between Raphael's legs. As he fell to the ground in agony, she yelled, "LEAVE THOSE NICE GIRLS ALONE!" out the window, but because she was too excited to remember to speak French, she said this in German[186] and ended up rather confusing everybody instead.

Whilst all of this was going on, Herr Bettelstein began to carefully pour all of the ice-cream toppings that they had from the first-floor window of the brasserie and down on to the rather discombobulated Raphael. Herr Bettelstein layered that man with chocolate sauce and whipped cream and chopped nuts and rainbow sprinkles and cherries before adding the final touch of an entire tub of sauerkraut whilst shouting, "YOU ARE NOT WELCOME IN MY BRASSERIE AT ALL, YOU MEAN MAN." He decided to translate it to German[187] and Spanish,[188] just to make sure that Raphael understood him, and then for good measure yelled at him in Klingon[189] as well.

It was then that things got rapidly worse for Raphael Gagnon.

....

186 *"LASS DIESE SCHÖNEN MÄDCHEN ALLEIN!"*
187 *"IN MEINER BRASSERIE SIND SIE ÜBERHAUPT NICHT WILLKOMMEN, SIE MÖCHTEN MANN."*
188 *"¡NO ERES BIENVENIDO EN MI BRASSERIE, HOMBRE MALO!"*
189 *"BLJEGHBE'CHUGH VAJ BLHEGH!"*

A row of first-years, lined up in the doorway of the plant shop, began to throw handfuls of compost at him. He stumbled furiously toward them but rapidly changed his mind when he saw the thick barricade that they'd built out of enormous potted plants and several handy sacks.[190] There was no way that he was getting into that shop without getting at least one plant stuffed up his nose. Or worse.

Instead, Raphael stood in the middle of the street and tried to remember what he was doing. He wiped strawberry sauce out of his right eye, chocolate sauce out of his left, wiped one arm clean of whipped cream and hazelnuts, and then tried to not touch the other, which had a substantial amount of chocolate-truffle-shaped bruises. He tried to ignore the rapidly swelling headache that he was developing, thanks to Edie's shoe falling on his head, and he also tried very hard to ignore the fact that he wasn't quite seeing straight anymore.

But as he stared down Edie and saw past her, to the end of the street, he realized that things were about to get worse.

----

190 Edie, contentedly: "Honestly, I am the *best* teacher."

A SCALE MODEL OF A BALLISTA

A line of girls had formed at the end of the street. They had been entrusted with a very particular task and they were determined to deliver it for Edie to the best of their abilities or die trying. Rose Bastable, who had been sent to join them, had pointed out that they probably shouldn't die because that would mean that they couldn't come to any more meals ever again. This irrefutable logic had persuaded the first-years to both Not Die and to also send Sethi and Sabia Gopal up to the château for reinforcements in the shape of a box full of sandwiches.[191] They had hidden the sandwiches behind the gatepost to the château, picked up their weapons, and then marched out onto the Rue de la Vérité.

Ah yes. Weapons.

Perhaps I should explain that part as well.

The first-years were armed with water pistols,[192] catapults,[193]

---

191 The fillings included chocolate spread, crisps, ham and cheese, and cheese and ham. The last two may sound very similar but Thea de Grazie will tell you that they are not.

192 A vital thing to take on holiday, I think you'll agree.

193 These might sound complicated but they are in fact very easy to make. All you need are some sticks, some elastic bands, the time-pressure provided

and in the case of Ayesha Cartwright, who was particularly interested in ancient history, an especially particularly convincing scale model of a ballista.[194] As they began to line up at the end of the street, several things happened in quick succession. The girls in the plant shop closed the door and retreated to the cellar. Herr Bettelstein pulled the windows of the brasserie shut whilst Frau Bettelstein bolted the front door. Madame Laurentis and her small band of helpers in the chocolate shop closed their front door and all of the windows before retiring to the safety of the storeroom where they began to taste-test the salted caramel toffees she had been working on.

"Perhaps you could just give me the painting," Raphael said as he slowly took all of this in. "I promise that I'll look after it. My client knows a lot about paintings. It will be safe, I promise you."

The small and quite irritating[195] girl swelled with indignation. "It will be safe where it *belongs*, and that is with us," she said with great meaning. "So I promise you this: You have one more chance. Leave now."

"You know I can't do that," said Raphael.

"Then you know what I must do," said the girl.

"Yes," said Raphael. He took a deep breath. "I would expect nothing less."

....

by a phone call from Edie Berger, and Good Sister Gwendolyn's excellent teaching skills.

194   A ballista is an ancient Greek weapon. It looks a little bit like a big catapult and it is very difficult to take on holiday with you. We had to have quite the conversation with customs about it.

195   This is Raphael's description and although it is not flattering, I do actually think it is quite mild after everything that he had gone through.

PISTOLS AND PUMPKINS AT DAWN

Edie studied Raphael with some satisfaction. The rules of war had meant that she had had to ask him to give up then, but a part of her would have been disappointed if he had said yes. In a way, his refusal to admit defeat had made her admire him a little bit more than she had done before. Even though he had made some very questionable decisions in his life and had some very questionable ideas about personal possessions, he was true to himself and that counted for a lot in her world.

It was because of this that she allowed him three whole steps without anything happening to him. Even Raphael himself looked confused when this happened. He stopped after the third and then looked at her and back at the row of silent girls who had watched all of this happen. He raised his eyebrows.

Edie smiled. She moved to the side so that she was out of the way. "First rank," she said. "Fire."

And then several things happened in quick succession.

The line of girls split in two, so that one stood in front of the other. The first row, which was armed with catapults and water pistols that had been loaded with the Bettelsteins' soup of the day,[196] fired everything that they had at Raphael. It was the shock of the moment more than anything that made him stumble back and skid on the piles of wet compost on the street around him. He fell to his knees and said something very rude.[197]

"Second rank," said Edie contentedly. "Fire."

The first row dropped to their knees to reload,[198] just as the second line and behind that, a particularly well-aimed ballista, fired. Raphael was soaked again, and then—although he could not quite believe that it was happening—hit in the stomach by a cauliflower. He said something very rude again[199] before hauling himself to his feet and storming forward toward them.

"First rank," said Edie. "Fire." A pumpkin flew over her head just as she finished speaking and smacked heavily into Raphael's shoulder, knocking him back down onto his knees. As they saw him fall, some of the girls from the plant shop opened their door to throw more compost at him whilst in

....

196 Tomato.

197 "BOILED BRUSSELS SPROUTS!"

198 You might wonder how such a thing occurred, for water cannot be conjured out of thin air. Isane Larsen had been stationed behind the shrubbery with buckets of water. She had hidden there until the first rank had fired, and then run out with her buckets and placed them at useful intervals between the girls so that they could reload their water pistols. She did not need to worry about getting shot, for she was quite small and nimble, and she did not need to worry about the people with catapults, for they had kept their ammunition in their pockets. And if that doesn't tell you of the importance of pockets, then I don't know what will.

199 "COLD PARSNIP SOUP!"

the distance, Frau Bettelstein stepped out from the café and launched some *apfelstrudel* at him.[200]

Edie knew that she didn't have much time for the next, and final, part of her plan. She looked around the street to make sure that everybody was in place. Calla and Hanna were still hiding behind Monsieur Abadie's bench, just where she had told them to wait,[201] and Rose Bastable was right where she should be at the château gate. As Ayesha and her small band of helpers launched a volley of turnips at Raphael, Edie looked over at Rose. "Are you ready?"

"I'm the best sprinter in the entire school," Rose said with some satisfaction. "Nobody can catch me. He won't get anywhere close."

"Sometimes I find you very annoying," said Edie. "But also, sometimes I think that you might be one of my favorite people that I have ever met."

Rose gave her a sudden, beautiful smile when she said that and for a heart-swelling moment, Edie felt as if it was just the two of them on the planet.

"Rose," said Edie. "My esteem for you is—"

Ayesha said, "PAY ATTENTION, EDIE."

Edie swung around to see Raphael almost on top of her. She darted back just as he reached out for the painting and skidded on a pile of whipped cream and pickled cabbage. He

....

200 Gloriously.

201 "Are you sure he won't see us?" Calla said when Edie explained this part of the plan.

    Edie nodded. "He won't notice anything but me," she said, "because all he wants to see is the painting."

rolled as he hit the ground and picked himself back up within seconds, to head straight for her. And even though every girl on the street was firing or throwing something at him, he barely seemed to notice. His complete and terrifying focus was on her.

Panicked, Edie reached underneath her jumper and produced a familiarly shaped package. She thrust it at Rose. "Give me yours!"

"What?" said Rose, staring at her.

"No time," said Edie. She swapped the two packages over. "Take the painting to the château. Take it now. You have to keep it safe! Run!"

Rose ran. Within seconds, she was halfway up the hill and heading straight toward the château.

And following her went Raphael.

ROSE BASTABLE, CHAMPION SPRINTER

Rose kept running. It was a task that Edie would have entrusted to nobody else and both of them knew it. She dodged past the hedges and the spaces where Odette herself had hidden so long ago, and headed straight for the front door. She did not wait to be let in but instead banged her hand loudly on it as she ran into the building and straight into the stomach of Good Sister Christine.

"Good evening, Rose," said Good Sister Christine as she calmly untangled Rose from herself. "I presume you have matters of great importance to share. Come with me. Good Sister June and Madame Berger are in the kitchen with the rest of the police and everyone else. You must tell us everything."

"That man is right behind me! We don't have much time."

A woman in the hall turned around to look at Rose. "The thief? He is coming here? Now?"

Rose nodded. "He's covered in compost and cabbage and quite a lot of ice cream toppings. If you don't see him, you'll hear him squelching up the path. Or you'll *smell* him."

The woman nodded. She snapped out three quick orders to

the policemen standing next to her, just as Good Sister Christine propelled Rose into the château kitchen. The room was full of more police and nuns and people, and eventually Good Sister Christine found Rose a seat next to Good Sister June.

Good Sister June wrapped her arms around Rose. "Are you all right? You're not hurt at all?"

"I am having the best night ever," Rose said with some feeling.

"We need you to tell us everything you know," said one of the policemen.

"Take a bit of this first, please," said Good Sister Honey, pushing some hot, buttery toast in front of Rose. "Nothing useful can be done on an empty stomach."[202]

Once she had eaten, Rose told them everything. She told them about how the girls had stolen the painting back from Raphael and how they had distracted him with fakes and then, when that hadn't worked, about how Edie had started a small cheese-themed riot to give them time to escape. When she finished this part of the story, a tall and smart-looking policewoman leaned forward. She gestured at the package that Rose had laid gently on the table next to her. "Do you have the painting now? Is this it?"

And before Rose could respond, somebody else did it for her. "Of course she doesn't," said a man standing in the corner of the room. "My daughter would never be that obvious."

---

[202] Truly, Good Sister Honey is the wisest of us all.

A CONFESSION

"I swapped it," said Edie. "Of course I did."

AN EXPLANATION

Sleight of hand is a fancy phrase for making people look at one thing while you do something else that they haven't noticed. It happens when people are doing card tricks or magic or producing a hidden Victoria sponge after they've told you that they're out of cake, and it relies on you seeing what you want to see. And what Raphael had wanted to see was the painting.

He had not, however, been able to see what had happened on the Rue de la Vérité before he got there. He had not seen Rose and Edie have a quick conversation and swap their packages over before he had gotten there. He had not realized that Edie had a fake package all along.

And so, when Edie and Rose swapped their painting-shaped packages right in front of him, Raphael Gagnon had not realized that he had been duped.

MIDNIGHT[203] IN PARIS

"And now we, ourselves, we have got the painting and they have got him," Edie said as she finished explaining. "He is going to run right into their hands and they are going to tie him up and send him to prison forever. Once that is all finished, Rose is going to tell them where to meet us, and all we have to do is be there for that. Which means! Ultimately! That I can give you a private guided tour of my beautiful city!"

She led Calla and Hanna between a final row of houses, before all of a sudden they came onto a wide and bright street full of cars and noise. "This street is called the Champs-Élysées," she said, grinning with satisfaction as she saw the looks on their faces. "It is one of the richest streets in Paris and I had to show it to you. I like it very much because we have done a lot of marches here and protests. It is a lot of fun! And there is always time for the things that I like. Namely, macarons! There is a shop on this street that makes the most

---

203 Technically it was about half past ten, but as I feel that is a very adult thing to say I am going to put it in the footnote and then go away and be old somewhere else.

perfect macarons ever! Tomorrow—if we survive tonight, my dear friends—I shall bring you here once more and we shall eat and eat and never leave!"

(As you may be able to tell by the amount of exclamation marks in that previous sentence, Edie was quite satisfied with the result of her plan.)

"But what about tonight?" Calla said calmly. She had lived the sort of life where her family could not often afford supper and so the shiny and expensive things in the nearby shop-windows were as distant to her as the moon. "I'm fairly sure we're still carrying a priceless painting and there are a *load* of things that could go wrong."

Hanna nodded and began to list them off in a helpful manner. "He could catch up with Rose and—"

"No," said Edie quite firmly, and her mind went back to the strange delight of that moment she'd had with Rose earlier. "Rose is a champion sprinter and the fastest in the entire school, faster even than Good Sister June when she sees a fresh Victoria sponge. She will not fail me. I do not think she would *ever* fail me. I would not have entrusted this so vital task to her if I had thought otherwise."

"She might get abducted by aliens," said Hanna. She started walking backward so that she could look Edie directly in the face. "Have you thought of that?"

"No, I have not," said Edie, carefully turning her friend back around so that she was facing the right way.

"If Rose does get abducted by aliens, then I think *everybody* will be more concerned with that than they are with a painting."

Edie nodded. "This is an important point. And now I am going to firmly change the subject." She gestured down the street and toward a tall white arch in the distance. It was in the middle of a roundabout full of traffic. "That building is the Arc de Triomphe and I have told Rose that this is where we shall wait for them. It is a perfect place to meet, for we shall be safe beneath it the entire time. It is the ideal place to hide. There are twelve roads that meet here so that means that there is a constant stream of traffic arriving from all directions. Nobody can get through to it without being spotted."

As they got closer, Calla and Hanna realized that she was right. There were no lane markings on the roundabout and all of the traffic looked like it might crash into each other at any second. The thought of anybody walking through all of that was almost impossible to comprehend.

"We're going to get squished," Hanna said with sonorous doom as she studied it.

Edie patted her fondly on the shoulder. "My little Hanna Banana, I do think that sometimes you forget that I grew up here. Nobody is going to be squished unless they make me squish them! We are going underneath the traffic! There is an underpass that leads through to the arch and we will be safe the entire time." She led the two of them toward the monument and down some stairs and into a tunnel. "I first came through here when I was five years old. Of course, I was not meant to be *technically* by myself in the middle of the city, but the metro system is surprisingly manageable at that age."

And then suddenly they were climbing back up to street level and beneath the arch itself. It was so enormous that they had to tilt back their heads to see all of it, and even then they couldn't quite take it in. They wandered slowly around the monument, looking at all of the carvings, before they headed for the middle of it to sit down and hide. Edie pointed at a marked-off area under the arch itself as they got closer. It was surrounded by low bollards connected to each other with a chain that came to about the height of their ankles. Something had been engraved on the floor while at one end, surrounded by flowers, a flame was burning.

"A grave," said Calla. "Isn't it?" She turned to Edie with her eyebrows raised. "I don't know the French, but there's one like this in my dad's graveyard. With the writing, I mean."

Edie nodded. "It is the tomb of the unknown soldier. It was somebody who died for their country but nobody knows who they were. To honor them and all of the other soldiers that died, the flame never goes out. My parents first brought me here when I was very young and told me all about it. I doubt they even remember, but I do. It is one of my favorite places in the entire city."

And then suddenly she stopped talking.

Because just opposite, with his eyes firmly fixed on her and a substantial amount of cabbage in his hair, was Raphael Gagnon.

ANOTHER CONFESSION

"I overheard everything," said Raphael. "Of course I did."

ANOTHER EXPLANATION

Raphael had been halfway up the hill when he realized that something was wrong. The first clue was that he had not been assaulted by anything for at least three minutes. Nobody had shot him with a tranquilizer dart, none of the ponds had transformed into a small child, and nobody had thrown compost at him, and that, more than anything, had told him to be cautious. Almost instinctively he had slowed down and squelched his way into a shadowy hiding place near the front door. It was close enough to see and hear what happened, but far enough away so that he had a chance that he might not be seen. He had spent months hiding in these gardens and working out how best to steal the painting. He knew every secret about this place.

It was because of this that when the police came out to catch him, they could not find him. Raphael had taken a deep breath and burrowed so deeply into the undergrowth around him that he became more hedge than man. He waited there until he was completely sure that the police had disappeared down the hill before crawling forward on his hands and knees until he was just outside the château itself. A row of parked cars was in front of him. He hot-wired[204] the nearest, a white-and-blue car that belonged to the police, and then drove it down the road that it had driven up only minutes earlier. As he navigated his way into the Parisian traffic, he turned on the police radio.

And heard everything.

---

204 *Hot-wiring* is a fancy word for when you start a car without having the keys, and if you don't have the keys, then you are usually stealing the car, which is precisely what Raphael was doing.

FACING DOWN THE DARKNESS

"Get behind me," Edie said to Calla and Hanna.

"You don't have to look so worried," said Raphael. He lifted up his hand to halt them. "I am not going to do anything awful to any of you, provided you just give me the painting. I have *total* justification in being awful after everything you have done to me, but I will not. I'm sorry that it has to be like this."

"I am not," said Edie. "I am not sorry about any of it. We cannot give you the painting. We will not."

"Well, I think that you must think about the fact that I am the police now," Raphael said serenely. He stood up and began to squelch his way over to the girls. "I drive the car, I put on the siren, and the people get out of my way. It is remarkable, really. It makes me think I could just arrest you now and nobody would have any problems whatsoever. You have stolen something that belongs to me, so I have complete justification to do so."

Edie glanced over to the underpass. It was so close. She wondered if they could make it.

"You won't make it," said Raphael. He moved closer. "What is it with you? Why can't you understand what's going on?

Why can't you realize that this is when you surrender? Do you not understand?"

"No," said Calla. She was unable to stop herself from smiling despite the fact that she was not enjoying this conversation in the slightest. "I actually think she doesn't understand at all. It's like a genetic impossibility for her."

Hanna glanced significantly at the road and then at Edie. "Tell me you have a plan that doesn't turn us into strawberry jam."

Edie didn't say anything.

She was suddenly very preoccupied with the car she had seen circle them three times now. She was fairly sure that it was being driven by Good Sister June. It was not the sort of thing that she had ever expected to see in Paris, and especially not when she had left Good Sister June in the kitchen at the château.

"By the way," said Hanna, "I don't think silently staring at the traffic is a plan."

Edie still didn't speak. She was too busy staring at the traffic on the roundabout because something else was happening. Not only was Good Sister June definitely driving one of the cars but none of them were turning off the roundabout or driving away. In fact, they were getting closer. If anything, it looked like they were about to turn up onto the curb and drive straight at the arch itself.

And then, suddenly, Edie realized something else.

All of the cars were being driven by nuns.

THE SOUND OF THE NUNDERGROUND

Here is the second-to-last reveal of this book.

When the police had left to capture Raphael and been somewhat unsuccessful in their endeavor, Good Sister June had
made a phone call. She had rung a woman called Sœur Chantal, who was the head of the Abbaye Convent in Paris.

Sœur Chantal was—and indeed *is*—a rather remarkable
nun. She is ninety-three years old and roughly the same size
and build as a stout golden retriever. She is also the head of
a network of nuns that is unofficially known as the Nunderground.[205] There are other names for it, of course, but I cannot tell you and you cannot ask Sœur Chantal, for she won't
tell you either. The Nunderground works best when not many
people know about it because its activities change the world
on a daily basis. The nuns provide shelter to the homeless and

---

205 The Nunderground was set up in 1919 by a nun named Sister Maria
Dawn, who realized how much her local community needed help after
the First World War. And so, every evening when the villagers went to
sleep, Sister Maria Dawn and her fellow nuns would creep out from their
convent and help tend crops and feed animals and do anything else that
was needed for their community to survive.

food for the hungry, assist children with their homework, and sometimes—when needed—help trap art thieves at national monuments in the middle of Paris.

It was not that Good Sister June *knew* that Raphael would make his way to the Arc de Triomphe. It was rather that she had the sneaking suspicion that wherever Edie was, trouble would soon follow. Sometimes it would be the good and beautiful kind of trouble but on a night like this, it would be the sort of trouble that might require a helping hand. And so she had called for the Nunderground, and they had come from all corners of the city to drive around the monument in case they were needed.

When Sœur Chantal realized what was happening, she beeped the horn of her very small and very yellow car and drove firmly toward the Arc de Triomphe itself. Within seconds, she was joined by a hundred other cars doing the exact same thing. All of the cars drove up to the fence and parked so tightly together that there was no hope of getting past them. Behind them, a layer of taller vans suddenly appeared to provide a further barrier.

Raphael flung a quick, wild look toward his car. It was boxed in. He wouldn't even be able to open the door. He turned then to check the underpass, but that was full as well. Not of cars, of course, but of people. The police were there, and alongside them were a blessing of nuns and a whole crowd of warlike schoolgirls. Good Sister Christine and Good Sister Honey stood next to Odette Berger, who was in turn surrounded by a group of familiar and fiercely protective faces. Rose Bastable, champion sprinter, still disheveled from her wild and record-breaking sprint through the château garden, locked eyes with Edie and waved. Maisie Holloway and Lucy Millais, best friends even though they didn't quite realize it yet, stood next to Sethi and Sabia Gopal, and in front of them was everybody else. Ellen. Claire. Ayesha. Katya Brookes. Sally Campbell. Jia Liu. A very sleepy Lily Maguire. It was a barricade built of everything wonderful about the School of the Good Sisters and Edie suddenly loved it very much. "You have to accept whatever comes, and the only important thing is that you meet it with the best you have to give," she quoted[206] as she turned back to face Raphael. "I am sorry, but I think this is it. You must do the right thing. Be the honorable man that I think you are underneath it all. Let us end this."

Raphael glanced toward the rapidly closing group of policemen and girls and then at the painting, still held tightly in Edie's arms. He suddenly looked very tired. "I did this for the painting. I am sorry. I just—I had a job to do. You got in the way of it. I did not mean any of it."

"I know," said Edie. "Neither did we."

Raphael held up his hands so that the policeman could handcuff them. "In a way, it is nice to know who has beaten me," he said as he was surrounded by the police. He glanced at Lucy and Maisie meditatively. "I recognize their faces. Those two, for example, threw the compost at me. Their aim is very good. You should put them in all the sports matches you wish to win. Oh, and that one—there, by the runner—she is the

----

206 This is a quote from a lady called Eleanor Roosevelt, whose favorite food was scrambled eggs. She thought they were eggcellent.

one who built that remarkable cauliflower-throwing contraption. She is most talented." He paused and then gestured with his cuffed hands in a particular direction. "But who are the two people over there—by your great-grandmother? I do not know them at all."

Edie looked over to where he had pointed. At first, she did not quite understand what she was looking at, until all of a sudden, she saw it. Or rather, them.

"They are my parents," she said.

A HURT THAT MAKES ITSELF KNOWN

And even though her parents were there, just on the other side of the monument, Edie Berger found herself unable to go to them. She had dreamt of this moment for years but now that they were there, she could almost not believe it. She felt sick and tired and happy and sad and none of it made sense. None of it. And that made it all feel worse.

So she stayed precisely where she was. She watched her parents and Odette start to talk to the police while Raphael was taken to the nearest police car. She watched Calla and Hanna be carried away by a crowd of adoring first-years, and the nuns slowly reversing away from the monument and driving off into the distant streets of Paris.

It was then that Good Sister June placed her hand on Edie's shoulder. "Hello," she said. "Are you all right?"

"No," said Edie. "I do not think that I am."

Good Sister June kept her hand precisely where it was. She glanced over at the police and then back at Edie, and saw the tight outline of the painting underneath her jumper. "Edie. Do you still have the painting?"

"Yes," said Edie. She reached in to produce the package and

gave it to Good Sister June. "Will you take it from me? I do not think I can hold it much longer."

Good Sister June took the painting. But she did not move.

Edie turned to look her in the eyes. "Why are my parents here?" she said.

"Because I called them," said Good Sister June. "The moment I heard that your grand-mère was offering us the château, I called them."

"But why?"

Good Sister June took a deep breath. "Because you miss them," she said.

A curious expression passed over Edie's face as she admitted the truth of this. "I do," she said. "But I do not know why it hurts so much to see them now. I do not understand why it hurts more. I think that maybe I should not hurt when my parents are right in front of me and yet I do. I do not know what to do."

"Be true to who you are," said Good Sister June. "Oh, Edie Berger, if you do nothing else, be true to that."

TOGETHER, FOREVER

Edie's reaction was not immediate. Nor was it even anything recognizable as a reaction. For a long time, Good Sister June wondered if she had gone too far or said the wrong thing.

But then suddenly Edie took a step forward.

And then she began to run.

Jean-Claude Berger was the first to see the wild-haired whirlwind heading his way. He had thought about this moment a thousand times since they had left Edie at the château, but he had never imagined it might be underneath the Arc de Triomphe, surrounded by a substantial number of nuns, schoolgirls, the police, his own grandmother, and one very penitent art thief.

But when Edie flung herself at him and Marianne, he realized that nothing could ever be as perfect as this. For a moment he could not figure out where he stopped and where his daughter began, or who was crying the most or the loudest, or how he had ever been away for so long. Holding Edie was like having his heart made whole.

Even if she did have surprisingly bony elbows.

Marianne was the first of them to speak, even though her

eyes were still full of tears. "You are so tall," she said as she studied Edie. She shook her head almost disbelievingly. "Have we really been away for so long? I remember you as small!"

"I *am* small," said Edie as she wrapped her arms around her father. A part of her had forgotten just how warm and solid he felt. It was like hugging a bear, but a wise and gentle and less-inclined-to-eat-you bear. "I am just *less* small than I was. And besides, you have been away for a long time and I have had *very* little clue as to where you have been! It is only natural that I change under the circumstances. You would not like it if I did not. Are you at home now? For how long? Are you staying?"

"For a long while," Marianne said lovingly. "And probably for longer than that. There are projects here that need us and we can do great things. We will be here until you go back to school and then you can come home for the holidays and bring your friends. All of them. Even the ones who keep talking about fish fingers."

Edie's heart skipped a little beat. She had been so caught up in the thrill of seeing Raphael captured and the painting saved, and the joy of having her parents so close to hand that she had almost forgotten the fact that she wasn't going back to school.

But she was nothing if not brave and so she took a deep breath. "Maman, there is something I must tell you about the school. Grand-Mère has decided that—"

"Hang on," said Marianne. "I think that somebody wishes to speak to us."

THE CONFESSION OF RAPHAEL GAGNON

Somebody did wish to speak to them. She was the chief of police and she had an unusual request. "I have an unusual request," she said, as she glanced back at the police car. "Mr. Gagnon would like to speak with you all before we take him away. It is not quite the thing that we normally do, but I think that, perhaps, this is not quite the most normal of situations."

"Of course we will speak with him," said Edie, rapidly deciding to focus on this instead of telling her mother about the whole not-going-back-to-school thing.[207] "This is a valuable educational experience. Will you bring my grand-mère over to join us?"

Within moments, they were gathered around the police car that contained Raphael. From somewhere, one of the policemen produced a folding chair for Odette to sit on. Edie came to stand next to her. "Are you okay with this?" she said. "You do not have to do it."

"I need to look him in the eye," Odette said calmly. She took

---

207 This is a direct quote from Edie herself.

Edie's hand in hers for a swift second. "But before all that, I need to thank you for everything you have done this night. I think I have not understood you for a long time, but now I do. You are amazing. Your friends are amazing. Your nuns dress a little bit like penguins, but they are also amazing. And so are you. Forgive me."

Edie exhaled.

Out of the corner of her eye she saw Maisie Holloway run past with a saucepan on her head.

"You do not need to say anything right now," said Odette.

"Honestly, I do not think that I can," said Edie.

"Are you ready?" said the police chief. She opened the car door and looked in. "Mr. Gagnon, they're here. Go ahead."

Raphael nodded and tried to move so that he could see them properly. It was not the easiest of things to do because he was handcuffed and the whipped cream and compost had begun to congeal on the car seat, but eventually he managed to position himself so that he was looking directly at everybody.

"I wish to apologize," he said formally. "I am sorry for what I have done to you all. I have expressed my regret to this small girl here and I think that we understand each other now. But I must express it to you, Madame Berger. I am so sorry. I would never have hurt that painting."

Odette studied him through narrow, disapproving eyes. "I accept your apology," she said coolly. "But still, I do not understand any part of this. What do you want with that painting in particular? I have others you could have taken from me and I would have let them go in a heartbeat. None of this had to happen."

"It would always have happened," said Raphael. "My client wanted that painting and so I was sent for it. That is what I do. I do not steal. I repatriate. I give people the things that have been stolen from them. This painting does not belong here and so I tried to take it back to its rightful home."

The police chief looked interested. "Who were you taking it to? You have to give us a name. Nobody knew this painting even still existed except Madame Berger. It's been one of the great mysteries of the art world."

"I do not have to do anything," Raphael said with some dignity. "You cannot throw any more cauliflowers at me, and I do not see any bags of compost anywhere for you to upend onto my head. There are no people upstairs to throw food at me, because there is no upstairs here, and there is definitely not anybody with a scale model of a ballista to catapult things at me."

Edie grinned. She put her fingers into her mouth and whistled loudly. All of the girls suddenly fell silent, stopped what they were doing, and turned around to look at her. Even Maisie Holloway, conscious that something important was happening, removed the saucepan from her head and paid attention. Good Sister Gwendolyn waved a fresh batch of darts at them. Ayesha Cartwright put down her bag of turnips. Rose Bastable rested her hands on her hips.

"We're *girls*," said Edie. "We don't need anything else but that."

Raphael studied her for a long time. A small lump of sauerkraut began to slide down his cheek. "Oh god," he said eventually. "I will tell you everything."

And he began with the name of his client.

IN WHICH THE WORLD STOPS TURNING

Her entire life had been on that train. She had lost it all. There was nothing left.

A DEFIANT, WELL-LIVED LIFE

Because Agathe Mercier had survived.

Somehow, against all odds, she had survived.

She did not know that she had survived at first. She was so close to death and saw nothing but darkness for weeks, and when she woke—properly, for the first time—she did not know who she was or even her name. It was only the quiet sound of her breath that had told her rescuers that a part of her was still alive. They had dragged her bloodied and broken body from the wreck of the train and then, startled by the flicker of life that still burned inside her, taken her to the doctor in the nearby village. And because she did not have papers or her memory, she took the name that they gave to her and lived that life instead of her own.

Her name changed every other week. She was Hester Braun for a while, taking the identity of a young member of the Resistance who had died, and then another week she was Anneli Weber, a distant cousin from Berlin whom nobody in the village had ever met. The people who found her on that first day kept her safe and moved her from family to family, along their great network of contacts, until at last she reached

Switzerland and a man who knew her real name. He did not expect to know the girl he was meeting on the mountains and bringing to safety, but when he saw the daughter of Kurt Mercier stumbling toward him, his heart had somersaulted and broken all at once.

His name was Michael Zimmerli, and he had been an assistant in an art gallery before the war. He had watched his manager buy and sell Kurt's paintings many times, and when he saw Agathe, his shock made him forget any attempt at security or safety and simply say, "I know who you are; I know about your father, and none of it matters. You are safe here, Agathe, you are safe."

And when he said that, a door finally opened inside of Agathe and brought her memories back to her.

She did not talk about them for a long while, though. It was not that she did not want to but she did not know where or even how to begin. There were not enough words in the world to capture what happened to her and so she took comfort in silence and memory. She dreamt of that first day that she and Odette had met, the two of them sharing shy and soft glances with each other beneath the paintings in the Louvre, and that night—the first of so many—when the two of them had talked for hours about nothing and everything all at once. And when those dreams ended, she started to think about how Odette's hair could catch the light, the way that it curled almost unconsciously when the air was damp, and how she never quite knew what to do with it.

Once she began to think like this, Agathe found that she could not stop. She spent days remembering the flat in

Munich, and how the three of them would paint into the early morning and then sleep until noon, only to wake up and do it all over again. The way that her father knew what was happening between her and Odette before she could quite put a name to it, and the way that he told her she did not need to put a word to it at all. "Some things do not need to be named," he had said. "Just be glad that they *are*."

And so one day, Agathe turned to the kind and gentle man at her side and told him everything. It took weeks for him to learn about it all, for they did not rush. She would sit down with Michael outside his house and wait until the sunset before she began. The beauty of it was just enough for her to let her story back into the world. She told it slowly and honestly, and although her words were soft, she recounted everything with a clarity that startled her. She told him about Odette, and her father, and their wild and desperate escape from Munich. She told him about the painting and how Kurt had made it so full of love and light and joy. She told him about the train and how the air had suddenly cracked with bullets. She told him about the way that she had stood up and walked toward the soldiers, and about how she had been ready to die, and then, when she had seen Odette fight her way back to her and appear at the window, her arm outstretched and her hand looking for hers, Agathe told him about how she had been suddenly so desperate to live.

And then on a night darker than the others, under a sky full of stillness and stars, she told him about the bullet and the way she had felt herself die; the way her body had folded and dropped to the floor, the way that she had watched it happen from somewhere else, the way that the world had darkened about her and the *peace* of it, the way that she remembered how it felt—the soft comfort of it—and then the roaring razor-sharp pain of being brought back to the world, the pain of living, of life without Odette at her side.

When she finished her story, Michael turned to her. He said, "You can use my spare room for as long as you like. I want you to know that I will help you find her. I will help you try." And he did. He brought Agathe stamps and paper to write letters to Paris, and he sat at her side as she tried to work out the street names and house numbers to send them to.[208] The two of them spent hours combing over newspapers together to look for mentions of Odette, but somehow they missed the quiet mention of the funerals of Hugo and Emilie Dupont and, of course, barely even noticed the marriage announcement of Odette Leroux to Luc Berger. After a year had passed and there was still nothing but silence and dead ends, Agathe had turned back to Michael and said, "I think Odette's dead."

And he said nothing and just held her and that was enough.

They were married six months later on a beautiful day in August. The sky was long and endless above them, bright blue and raw with heat, and Agathe wore a dress that was the same soft cream as the canvases her father had painted on, and a wreath of flowers in her hair in memory of Odette. They left a chair empty for each of them at the ceremony and when

---

208 There were thousands of people across Europe doing the same thing. The war had torn families apart and sent them all over the world. And some of them found each other and some of them did not.

it came to making the speeches at the evening reception, Michael told their guests about Kurt, and Agathe told them about Odette, and they never stopped talking about them in all the years since. Their family grew up knowing the stories of Munich and of Kurt and Odette, and so did their grandchildren and their great-grandchildren, two of them living in Salzburg, and another in Innsbruck, but all of them close enough to visit Michael and Agathe on the weekend for *kaffee und kuchen*[209] and all of the hugs in the world.

When Michael died, they buried him high in the mountains in the same place where he had met Agathe all those years ago. She led the tributes to him and told their story at the funeral, talking as much to the mountains and the clouds as she did the people, for if there was one thing Agathe had learned, it was that telling the stories of people mattered. And so she built a small cabin up there on the mountainside so she could continue to tell his story to the hikers and the climbers who bought a hot meal or a coffee from her, and she tended the small and sweet Alpine roses that she had planted over his grave, and once all of that was done she watched the sunset with her husband at her side and talked to him as if he was still there.

One day, almost by accident, one of her customers left a newspaper behind as he went to climb the mountain. She did not get much in the way of news up in her high and lonely

---

209 This is German for "coffee and cake," and it is a most important phrase to learn. Another important German phrase is *Dein Kuchen schmeckt gut*, which means "Your cake is delicious."

cottage and so she read it with interest, sitting out on the veranda so that she could spot the hiker as he came back down the mountain. And as she read it, she came across an article about her father and his paintings.

After all of these years, there he was.

It was as simple as that.

WHAT THE ARTICLE SAID

There are many artists who did not survive the war. Kurt Mercier was one of them. Known for his bohemian style and his rich and lavish sense of color, he was murdered by the Nazis in the early days of the conflict. Some of his work, however, survived and is among the most prized artwork on the planet. Much of it has been found since the war, but one painting remains missing. It is perhaps the most important one of all.

Les Roses Blanches.

LOVE IS LOVE IS LOVE

Les Roses Blanches.

Three words. That was all it took to make the years fall away. Suddenly she was sitting in the flat with Odette at her side. The two of them had been smiling and laughing about something that had happened that day, and Kurt had reached out for his oils. "No," he had said, when they noticed what he was doing. "Don't look at me—don't even remember that I exist. I just want to capture this. For me, stay where you are. Stay *how* you are."

It felt like minutes. Agathe knew that it must have taken longer, hours perhaps, for her father to finish working, but it felt like minutes. Every now and then Odette would steal a quick look at her, and she would feel her fingers intertwine with hers, and when Kurt stood up to open the curtains and let the dawn light in, neither of them quite noticed until he said, "Thank you, I love you both—so much—" and went off to sleep until the afternoon.

He left the canvas on the table, weighted down on the corners to let it dry, and Odette was the first to look at it. Her eyes had widened, and almost instinctively she had reached out for Agathe to come and join her. And so she did. Agathe walked over to her side and looked down at the painting.

"Oh," she said. "Oh—yes."

TO HOPE IS DIVINE

Agathe read that article until her finger was black and smudged from running along the printed paper. Her thoughts felt like bullets. People collected her father's work. He had not been forgotten. His paintings were precious and valued things.

And *Les Roses Blanches* was still missing. People had looked everywhere for it over the years. Some of them thought that it might have been destroyed after the war whilst others had never stopped believing that it might still be out there. There was a theory that it might be in France, based on a story that one cleaner had told another, and Agathe decided to start there.

But theories could not be investigated from mountains, nor could they be investigated alone. She needed help, and so she found a man called Raphael through one of Michael's old art contacts and arranged a meeting with him in a bland and nondescript café in the middle of the city. She explained the situation to him briefly and discreetly, but he was the sort of person who understood what that meant. He set off that night, and every morning since, Agathe had looked down the mountain in the hopes that she would see him returning with the painting in his arms.

And one morning, she saw something that she did not expect.

A helicopter had landed on a large patch of grass, just below her house, and several small figures were in the process of getting out. Some of them were dressed in black and white; two of them kept pausing to look at the plants that dotted the path, and three of them were substantially smaller than the others. One had yellow hair as bright as the sunflowers that Agathe planted each year, another was dark-haired and carrying a book,[210] whilst the other one had hair as wild as the storm clouds that sent thunder and lightning to the valleys below. Once the smaller figures had moved away from the helicopter, a final figure disembarked. She was old—so old—and had a cane at her side that she used to support herself as she walked forward.

Agathe sat down at the front of her house to watch them. She could not quite understand who they were or what they were doing on her mountain. She had served coffee and cake to tourists and hikers from all over the world for years now, and she understood them. Hikers looked like hikers. Climbers looked like climbers. But these people were neither, and that made them interesting.

The group started to head up the path up toward her home. One of the women, the tiny one with white hair and a walk so graceful that it made Agathe yearn to paint her, was at the

....

210 *The School at the Chalet* by Elinor M. Brent-Dyer.

back of the group. Two of the girls stayed with her whilst the one with bright yellow hair was busily chatting to the other women. As they got closer, Agathe started to hear snatches of their conversation. They spoke in English and kept referring to the adults as "Good Sisters," and that told Agathe that they were nuns. But not all of them. Not the girls and definitely not the woman at the back of the group.

When the group got within earshot, one of the nuns called out, "Are you Frau Zimmerli?" she asked. Her voice was polite and friendly. "Do you mind if we come and say hello in person? We've come a long way to meet you. I hear your Victoria sponge is exquisite. I've read all of your Tripadvisor reviews."

A thousand questions formed inside Agathe's head and none of them made sense. She settled instead for nodding and watching them walk into her garden. For a moment, the woman at the back of the group paused—just froze—and looked at her, before continuing to make her slow way up the path. Her cane tapped out a soft rhythm against the stones, casting a spell.

Agathe said, "Are you here for *kaffee und kuchen*? Coffee and cake? Before you climb the mountain? I can have some soup on ready for when you come back, if you like."

The woman at the back took a step forward. "I thought you were dead," she said. "For so long, I thought it. I *knew* it."

And suddenly Agathe understood.

"Oh, my love," she said. "Come home, at last, come home."

A FINAL THREAD

And so, in the twilight of their lives, Agathe and Odette were together again. It did not matter that Agathe's hair was white now or that Odette could not walk without her stick at her side, for the two of them were still the same people, and that was what mattered. They told each other about the lives they had lived and when they finished speaking, they looked at each other and felt their love come back to them as though it had never left.

That night, Agathe insisted that the others stay with them rather than fly back to Paris, and when she began to fry bacon and potatoes together for dinner, nobody could bear to say no. Hanna and Calla and Good Sister June carried the table outside while Good Sister Paulette and Edie found crockery and cutlery.[211] Odette stayed in the kitchen with Agathe and

---

[211] You may be wondering where Marianne and Jean-Claude Berger are, and so I have put in a footnote to tell you because I am the terribly helpful type. They had stayed in Paris to look after everybody there and tell them inspiring stories before bedtime. Besides, as Marianne herself had said, Edie and her friends had done all the work to reunite Odette and Agathe. It was right that they should be there to witness it.

every now and then, the two of them would pause from their cooking and simply hold each other in the middle of the soft evening light.

When the meal was done, and the others had tactfully found somewhere else to be, Odette told Edie that she had an apology to make to her. "I was wrong," the older woman said quietly. "I think this school of yours brings nothing but good. It has brought Agathe and me back together, and it has brought you back into my life in a way that I thought would never happen. It has taught you how to be true to yourself, and it has reminded me of the very same. You can go back to the School of the Good Sisters with my blessing. I should not have threatened to take it away from you. I am sorry."

Edie took a deep breath. She let it out. Behind her, she heard Hanna talking to Agathe about the Moomins while in the distance, Good Sister Paulette was showing Calla how to fix something on the helicopter. It was perhaps the most perfect combination of sounds that she had ever heard, and the thought of continuing to hear all of that for as long as she wanted left her unable to speak. She could not find the words.

And then, after a while, she realized that moments like this didn't need words.

They just needed each other.

ACKNOWLEDGMENTS

Thank you to Bryony Woods for believing in what *How to Be True* (and in me) could be from day one, and for making it all happen with such skill and brilliance (and puns). Thank you to Alli Hellegers for being such a supportive dream to work with, and thank you to Laura Godwin and all of the wonderful team at Henry Holt who have helped in getting Edie's story into the world. A special thank-you to Flavia Sorrentino for that cover, which captures my heart every time I look at it.

Thank you to Francesca Arnavas (owner of the original Arturo and Ginevra), Alison Baker, Clémentine Beauvais, Claire Boardman, Thy Bui, Roberta and Enya Echarri, Jacqueline and Nigel Grant (herluppalah!), Carmen Haselup, Mélanie McGilloway, Liz Osman, Jefferson Toal, Clara Vulliamy, Yu-Hua Yen, and all the lovely reviewers, blogger, librarians, and readers who have supported the School of the Good Sisters from the start. You make my dreams come true every single day.[212]

And last but by no means least, thank you to my eternally wonderful family. Let's go out for tea.

....

212 I think you're pretty fab.